Revved for Danger!

Frank and Joe found Jessica sitting on her motorcycle and talking to Grant Tucker, the hot-rod show promoter.

"Jessica doesn't like to be spied on," Grant announced to the Hardys when they approached. "I told her I brought you in to find out who was causing the accidents."

"I'm sorry we couldn't tell you the real reason we were here," Joe said to Jessica, "but people might not—"

From behind him, Joe heard the roar of a powerful engine. It was becoming louder. He glanced over his shoulder and froze in horror.

A bright blue 4x4 truck was coming straight toward them. Joe gaped in amazement when he saw that there was no driver at the wheel. In another moment they would all be crushed!

The Hardy Boys Mystery Stories

Available from MINSTREL Books

FEAR ON
WHEELS

FRANKLIN W. DIXON

PUBLISHED BY POCKET BOOKS

New York   London   Toronto   Sydney   Tokyo   Singapore

This book is a work of fiction. Names, characters, places and incidents are either the product of the author's imagination or are used fictitiously. Any resemblance to actual events or locales or persons, living or dead, is entirely coincidental.

A MINSTREL PAPERBACK *ORIGINAL*

A Minstrel Book published by
POCKET BOOKS, a division of Simon & Schuster
1230 Avenue of the Americas, New York, NY 10020

Copyright © 1991 by Simon & Schuster
Cover artwork copyright © 1991 by Paul Bachem
Produced by Mega-Books of New York, Inc.

ISBN: 0-671-69277-1

First Minstrel Books printing June 1991

10 9 8 7 6 5 4

THE HARDY BOYS MYSTERY STORIES is a trademark of Simon & Schuster

THE HARDY BOYS, A MINSTREL BOOK and colophon are registered trademarks of Simon & Schuster

Printed in the U.S.A.

Contents

1 The Flying Skulls Arrive

"Wow! A hot rod show," Joe Hardy whispered to his brother, Frank. "I'd like to ride one of those cool motorcycles up a jump ramp." Joe's blue eyes were always on the lookout for a challenge, and his muscular six-foot frame was quick to respond.

Frank laughed and replied, "Cool your jets, Joe. Let's see what Grant Tucker wants us to do for him first."

Frank and Joe Hardy followed the receptionist into an office of the Bayport Arena. Frank, who was tall and dark, paused for a moment to glance out the picture window. Down below, a big semi was pulling into the parking lot. On its trailer were half a dozen gleaming hot rods, in colors

1

that ranged from deep metallic blue to brilliant yellow gold.

"Mr. Tucker?" Frank said, turning to look at the man rising from his desk chair.

Nodding in reply, the man shook Frank's and Joe's hands. Tucker was short and stocky, with wide shoulders. His biceps strained the sleeves of a black T-shirt with Tucker Hot Rod, 4x4, and Motorcycle Show printed on it in orange and green letters.

"I'm Frank Hardy, and this is my brother, Joe. We've been hearing a lot about your show. It sounds great."

Grant Tucker waved them toward two chairs, and the Hardys sat down. "I don't know if there's even going to be a show," Tucker said, frowning. "We've got a problem."

"What kind of problem?" asked Joe, pushing back his blond hair. "Something we can help with?"

"I don't know," Tucker replied. "I hope so. I'm told you guys are terrific detectives." Tucker had heard from a contact in Bayport of the Hardys' reputation as investigators. Although Frank was only eighteen and Joe seventeen, they had already cracked many local cases and had solved mysteries in some far-off places, too.

"What do you think about this?" Tucker asked. He picked up a piece of paper and handed it to the brothers. Frank took it and held it so that Joe could read it, too. It appeared that the words had

2

been cut out of a book or magazine and pasted on the sheet of paper. It read, Grant Tucker—Pay $250,000 by Saturday night or more accidents will happen to your show.

"It's an extortion note," Joe said. "When did you get this?"

Tucker's face hardened. "This morning," he answered. "At first I just tossed it in the wastebasket. Then I decided it wouldn't be smart to ignore something like this. Two hundred fifty thousand bucks. They must be crazy! Who do they think I am?"

Frank leaned forward in his chair and said, "Maybe they think you're the country's leading promoter of hot rod and motorcycle shows. That's right, isn't it?"

"We've been listening to your commercials," Joe added with a grin.

Tucker straightened up and walked over to the window. "Who hasn't?" he said with his back to them. "My company spends more money on air time than some countries spend on their armies. In this game, publicity is the only way we keep going."

He fell silent. Then he turned around and pounded his fist into his palm. "Just when I was getting a big break, this had to come up. Do you realize that Saturday's show is scheduled to be on television live that night? Do you know what that could mean for us? But if the TV people hear about this threat, they might get spooked and

3

pull out. That's why I called you guys. What do you think? Can you help me?"

Frank glanced over at Joe, then said, "We'll do our best, Mr. Tucker."

"You can count on us," Joe added, his eyes flashing.

"Great," the promoter said. "But call me Grant. Okay, where do we start?"

"The note says 'more accidents' could happen," Frank pointed out. "Does that mean there have already been some?"

Tucker sat down at his desk, picked up a pen, and began to draw circles on a memo pad. "That's a good question," he replied. "In a show like this, there will always be a few accidents. The cars and bikes take a lot of hard treatment, and so do the performers. But since last month, we've had more and more things go wrong. Too many to be a coincidence."

"Can you give us some examples?" Joe asked.

"Sure. The other day, the knob on Keith Helm's stick shift came off in his hand as he was driving. No big deal, you might say, but when your engine's turning six or seven thousand revolutions per minute, a missed shift can mean you overrev and blow the engine. That same day, Bruce Sears found both his front tires flat. One, okay, it happens now and then. But both at the same time? Give me a break!"

"Were the tires punctured?" Frank asked.

4

Tucker shook his head. "Nope. No sign of that. Sometimes tires have leaky valves, but in this case I think somebody tampered with them."

"Could these incidents be someone's idea of a practical joke?" Joe asked. "They don't sound very dangerous, after all."

"Practical jokes? No way," Tucker replied. "I don't think a loose bolt on a steering arm is very funny, do you? Keith's lucky he spotted it. If he hadn't, he could have found himself going a hundred miles an hour with no way to steer. I'm telling you, if these accidents—or whatever you want to call them—don't stop, someone's going to get killed."

"Have you done anything to try to find out who's behind all this?" Joe asked.

The promoter cracked a smile. "Sure," he replied. "I called you guys. But seriously—"

The telephone rang. Tucker picked it up and muttered into it, then held up one finger to tell the Hardys that he wouldn't be long.

"What do you think, Frank?" Joe asked in a low voice. "It looks like an inside job, doesn't it?"

Frank pushed his brown hair out of his eyes. "It sure does. We'll have to check out their security, anyway. Although it's hard to imagine an outsider wandering freely around a bunch of valuable cars. Somebody would be bound to notice and ask him what he's doing."

Tucker hung up the phone. "That was a guy

5

you'd better keep an eye out for—Bob Morgan. He's an ace reporter for *Motorsports* magazine. I wish I knew why he's sniffing around here."

"Could he have heard about these so-called accidents?" asked Joe.

"I sure hope not, but it wouldn't surprise me. He's always on the lookout for a juicy story. Anyway, what was I saying?"

"You were starting to tell us what you've done about tracking down the guy who's causing all the trouble," Frank replied.

Tucker picked up his pen and started turning it over in his fingers. "Not all that much," he admitted. "I've had to be really careful. I can't take the chance of messing up this TV deal by drawing attention to what's been going on. This has got to look like a respectable operation. I couldn't go around asking questions, because I didn't want *anyone* to know. That's why I'm counting on you guys to do your job quietly."

"We'll have to work undercover," Frank pointed out. "Have you thought about how you're going to introduce us to the people who work for the show?"

"You're a little young to be with the TV network," Tucker replied. "And you probably don't have the technical experience to join the crew. Wait, how about this? A couple of months ago, Damon Stafford, our press agent, left to take another job. Since then, I've been handling press relations for the show by myself. What if I tell people I'm training you two to take over some of the media work? That'll give you a good excuse for hanging around and asking lots of questions."

"Good idea," said Frank. "We can work out the details later. But first, we'd better be clear on exactly what you want us to do. This guy who is trying to extort money from you—do you want us to stop him? Expose him? Pay him off?"

"Listen, you're the detectives," Tucker replied. "You do what you have to do. If you can discover who it is, we'll take it from there. The only thing I care about right now is Saturday's show. I want it to go off without any major hitches. Whatever it takes to make that happen, that's okay with me."

"What if it looks like paying him off is the only way to keep the show on schedule?" Joe asked. "After all, today is Thursday, which doesn't leave us much time. Can you come up with the money?"

"I don't know. I'd have to borrow it from somewhere."

"Joe doesn't mean paying him off and leaving it at that," Frank explained. "We've found that setting up a payoff can be the best way to trap an extortionist."

Tucker nodded. "That makes sense."

"Do you have any suspicions about who the extortionist is?" Frank asked.

Tucker pushed his chair back from the desk and stood up. "You bet I do," he said, fists on hips. He dug through a stack of papers, pulled out a newspaper clipping, and slid it across the desk to the Hardys.

Frank picked it up, glanced at it, and passed it on to Joe. "Fat Dave?" Frank asked. "The guy who heads up that motorcycle club over on the north side?"

"The Flying Skulls," Tucker replied. "And 'gang' is a better word for them than 'club.'"

"Fat Dave was interviewed on TV a few weeks ago," Joe said. "He was saying that forcing motorcycle riders to wear helmets is un-American."

"They interview him anytime there's a story about motorcycles," Tucker said. "Fat Dave and the Flying Skulls love to get on television. If I could use the media as well as that dude, this would be the biggest bike and rod show in the world."

"Why do you suspect the Flying Skulls are behind the accidents and extortion?" Frank asked.

"Fat Dave's newest campaign is to try putting me out of business. He's got this idea that since I'm making a profit from a motorcycle show, I owe something to bikers like him and his gang. That's not the beginning, though. He's had it in for me for a while. When I was a kid, I was in a motorcycle club that didn't get along with the

Skulls. Fat Dave can't forget that. Then, a couple of years ago, I didn't hire one of his buddies to perform in the show. The last time we did Bayport, he came around and called me some names."

"What happened?" asked Frank.

Tucker grinned. "I called him some names back, he threw a punch, and I did the same to him. The only reason I'm still walking around is that he didn't have any of his buddies with him to help him out."

"So instead of beating you up, he's trying to wreck your show," Joe said. "Is that what you figure?"

"You got it," Tucker replied. He started pacing back and forth behind the desk.

"One thing I don't understand," Frank said. "Joe and I were talking while you were on the phone, and at this point it seems as if the accidents have to be an inside job. You'd know it if some of Fat Dave's guys were hanging around and tinkering with the cars, wouldn't you?"

"Sure, the security crew would recognize them," Tucker said. "I may not have the best security in the world, but it's pretty good."

"If you're right about Fat Dave and the Skulls," Joe said, "it's possible that somebody in your show is working with the gang."

Tucker looked at Joe. "I hear you, but I can't believe it. Why would anybody in the show want

9

to destroy it? Especially now, when things may be starting to happen for us in a big way? It doesn't make any sense."

"The Skulls could have bribed somebody," Joe said. "Or threatened him."

"And remember," Frank added, "not all of the people in the show have the same stake in it. Will it make any difference to one of the guards or mechanics, for instance, if this TV coverage ever happens?"

"Maybe not," Tucker said slowly. "But if the show has to fold, we're all out of a job. Besides, we're not just a business, we're a family. Like any family— Hey, what's that?"

From outside the window came a loud rumbling sound. Frank noticed a glass on Tucker's desk starting to vibrate. The sound grew louder and louder. Tucker rushed to the window. Frank and Joe jumped up and crossed the room to stand next to him.

"Oh, great!" Tucker exclaimed. "That's all I need."

Frank looked down at the parking lot. The arena ticket office was just below the window. Heading toward it, in ranks of four abreast, were forty or fifty big motorcycles. Their riders were wearing torn, faded jean jackets, studded black leather gloves and belts, and metal helmets that looked like props from an old war movie. The people on the ticket line scattered as the pack drew closer and stopped.

Frank craned his neck to see the emblem sewn on the back of one of the denim jackets. But he already knew what he would see—a grinning skull with wings sprouting from each side. The Flying Skulls had arrived.

2 Run of Bad Luck

Joe glanced over at Grant Tucker. The promoter's fists were clenched, and his face was growing red.

"I'm not taking any more of this!" Tucker shouted. He whirled around and started for the door.

Joe followed him and grabbed his arm, but Tucker brushed him off. Frank jumped ahead and stood in front of the door.

"Out of my way." Tucker tried to push Frank aside.

"Uh-uh," Frank said, shaking his head from side to side. "You asked us to help you avoid bad publicity, remember? What kind of publicity will you get if you go down there and start throwing punches?"

"You got any better ideas?" Tucker demanded. "Those guys are out to ruin me. They're scaring off my ticket buyers. I can't let that happen."

Joe returned to the window. "Hey," he called. "Come take another look."

"What now?" Tucker grumbled, but he let Frank lead him back across the room. Down below, the gang of bikers was surrounded by a crowd of curious spectators.

"There's your answer," Joe said. "All those people down there think the Skulls are part of your show. They want to meet them and get their picture taken with them. So give them what they want."

Frank snapped his fingers. "That's it! Listen, Grant, I know shows often keep a block of good seats set aside for last-minute VIPs. Do you?"

The promoter hesitated. "Well . . . sure. But you two can watch from backstage."

"It's not for us," Frank continued. "I've got a plan for dealing with the Skulls. Back me up on this, okay?"

Tucker looked doubtful, but all he said was, "I hope you know what you're doing."

Frank led Joe and Tucker downstairs. When they came outside, some of the Flying Skulls recognized Tucker. They started shouting and making catcalls. Some of them got off their bikes and began to walk slowly toward him. The spectators, apparently sensing the tension, backed away.

13

Frank realized that he had to act quickly, before the situation got out of hand. "Come on," he muttered to Joe. "There's Fat Dave, over on the left."

Frank saw the bikers' leader leaning against his parked motorcycle. His thumbs were tucked into the pockets of his jeans. He looked as if he weighed over two hundred pounds, most of it under his wide silver-studded belt. Fat Dave wore his brown hair tied back with a leather thong, and his beard reached down to his chest. His eyes were hidden behind a pair of dark glasses.

"Hi, Dave," Frank called out as they drew closer. The biker straightened up, ready for anything. "I'm Frank Hardy, and this is my brother, Joe. Thanks for coming by so quickly."

Half a dozen bikers surrounded the Hardys, pressing in closely.

"What are you talking about, 'coming by so quickly'?" Dave asked.

"You got Grant's message, didn't you?" Frank continued. "About the passes for tomorrow night? How many do you figure you'll need?"

Joe jumped in. "Here's the plan, if it's okay with you. We'll rope off part of the parking lot right over there, near the main entrance, and set aside a block of seats down front. You and your club members show up a little before show time, park your hogs, and make an entrance as a group."

"But we'll need to know how many seats to put

14

aside," Frank added. "It's opening night, and sales are going well. We don't want to overbook."

"Hold it," Fat Dave said. "I don't like people to talk at me too fast. Who are you dudes, and whose idea is this plan you're talking about?"

"We're Frank and Joe Hardy," Frank replied. "We're going to be helping Grant with public relations, dealing with the press, stuff like that. And this is Grant's way of showing his respect for the traditions of motorcycle clubs."

Fat Dave's lips curved into a smile. "I get it. Okay, tell your boss we accept. But he's crazy if he thinks he can buy off the Flying Skulls with a bunch of free passes. All he's doing is renting us for the evening."

The biker climbed onto his motorcycle, kicked the starter lever, and gunned the engine. Frank coughed as blue smoke billowed up in his face. Through the haze he could see Fat Dave's grin. The other Skulls were starting their machines, too.

"How many passes?" Joe shouted over the racket. "We need to know."

Fat Dave looked around and shrugged. "A hundred," he shouted back. Then he raised his hand over his head, swung it around once, and pointed forward. All the motorcycles began to move at the same moment. The spectators drifted back to the ticket line.

Tucker had stayed away from Fat Dave the whole time. When the cyclists had roared away, he came over to Frank and Joe and said, "What do you know? It worked. Now all we have to worry about is what they'll do at tomorrow's show."

"Not quite," said Frank. "We also have to worry about catching your extortionist and stopping these accidents. Do you have time to take us around and introduce us to a few people? The sooner we get to work on this case, the better."

"Sure, let's go."

Tucker led Joe and Frank across the parking lot to a loading dock. The big overhead doors were open. A uniformed guard sitting near the door glanced up from his newspaper and started to say something. Then he noticed Tucker, nodded, and went back to his paper.

A few moments later, the Hardys and Grant entered a huge room with cinder-block walls. It smelled of oil and exhaust fumes. Joe paused to look around. Dozens of hot rods and customized 4x4 trucks were parked on the cement floor. Most of them had their hoods up, but only a few mechanics were drifting from one to another, tools in hand.

"Not that much activity today," Tucker explained. "We give all the cars their final tune-up tomorrow, just before the show." He glanced around, then called out, "Jessica. Hey, Jessica, over here."

Across the room, Joe saw a girl with shoulder-length blond hair start toward them. Her black jeans, long-sleeved black T-shirt, and black cowboy boots gave her a tough, boyish look. But when she came closer, her face seemed almost childish. Her eye makeup made her dark eyes look huge.

"Jessica," Tucker said, "meet Joe and Frank Hardy. They're going to be giving me a hand with press relations. Could you take them around to meet the gang?"

"Sure, Grant," she replied. "I'd be glad to."

Tucker turned to the Hardys and added, "Jessica is one of our big stars. She can do just about anything with a motorcycle except make it sit up and beg, and I bet she's working on that. Right, Jess?"

"You bet," she replied.

"You're Jessica Derey?" Joe asked. He knew he must sound like an awestruck fan, but he couldn't help it. "I saw your Leap of Death on television," he added. "When you jumped your bike through those two turning propellers, I couldn't believe it."

Jessica laughed. "I couldn't, either," she said. "Afterward I went to my dressing room and stared at the mirror for a long time, just to make sure I was still alive. Then I went hunting for Grant, to give him a piece of my mind for talking me into a stunt like that."

"The audience loved it," Grant said, patting her shoulder. "And don't worry, I won't ask you to do it again. We've got it on tape, anyway." He turned to Joe and Frank and added, "Why don't you check in with me later?"

As he walked away, Jessica smiled and said, "I didn't catch what Grant said about your jobs."

"He called it press relations," Frank said, "but I think it's going to be more like damage control. For instance, Grant told us about a string of recent accidents that seem suspicious. He's worried that if the news gets around, people might decide the show is jinxed."

"We're supposed to help see that the story doesn't get around," Joe added quickly.

"It's just a run of bad luck," Jessica said.

"Have any of these accidents happened to you?" asked Joe.

"Not yet," she replied with a laugh. "I guess I should knock on wood when I say that, shouldn't I? But I'm not superstitious. Come on, let's go meet some of the guys."

As they started across the room, Frank said, "How did you get into motorcycle stunt riding? It's a pretty unusual line of work."

"Unusual?" Jessica repeated, smiling. "I like that. I call it weird, myself. But it's in the blood. My dad and mom were both bikers, out in California. After my sister and I came along, Dad traded his Harley for an old BMW motorcycle with a two-seater sidecar. It was a little wheeled thing that looked like a torpedo, fastened to the side of the motorcycle. People always waved at us when we went past. I guess that got me used to having an audience."

They turned into a wide corridor that led from the work area to the floor of the arena, where Joe noticed two men talking. One of them, in stained overalls and heavy work boots, had black hair that hung low on his forehead and thick black eyebrows that almost met in the middle. The other, a tall man with brown hair, was wearing expensive loafers, jeans, and a pale blue T-shirt with a picture of a Grand Prix motorcycle and under it the words I Climbed Pikes Peak.

The man with brown hair looked up as they approached and nodded to them.

"Hi, fellows," Jessica called. "This is Frank and Joe Hardy. They just signed on to do press stuff." She gestured to the brown-haired man and said, "Meet Keith Helm, the Dragging King of the Quarter-Mile. And this is Matt Nazer, our crew chief."

After a round of handshakes, Joe said, "Grant just mentioned your name, Keith. Something about a gearshift knob coming off?"

Keith looked surprised. "He told you about that? I thought he was trying to keep our little jinx under cover."

"He is," Joe explained. "Frank and I are going to help him do it, by keeping the press looking the other way."

"You've got your work cut out for you," Keith

said, grinning. "That reporter Bob Morgan was poking around a little while ago. He doesn't miss much."

"According to Jessica, these accidents are just a run of bad luck," Frank said. "But Grant gave me the feeling that somebody's out to damage the show. What do you guys think?"

"I don't know anybody here who'd want to hurt the show," Matt replied. "We're all in it together."

"Yeah," Keith said. "Accidents come with the territory."

"Well, I've got too much work to do to stand around gabbing," Matt said. "See you later." Keith said goodbye, and the two turned away and walked toward the work area. Joe noticed that Matt limped as if his right leg were in a cast.

"Matt was a top stunt rider, one of the best," Jessica said in a low voice. "Then, a few months ago, a stunt went bad on him. He came out of the hospital with a knee that doesn't bend. That was it for his career. You can't ride a motorcycle with a stiff leg."

"Gee, that's rough," Joe said. "Don't they make artificial knee joints these days?"

Jessica shook her head. "There's some problem with that. I don't know what. He doesn't like to talk about it. Oops, car coming—clear the way."

Three crewmen were pushing a customized candy-apple red roadster toward the arena. Joe admired the exposed engine, a big V-8. The shiny chrome air cleaners atop its six carburetors caught the light and seemed to glow. The man at the wheel, who was almost as blond as Jessica, nodded to her and the Hardys as the car glided past. As the car neared the arena entrance, the driver raised his right hand, then dropped it. The crewmen stepped back as the unmuffled engine roared into life. The roadster shot forward as if it had a rocket under the rear end.

"That Deuce really moves," Jessica said.

"Deuce?" asked Frank.

"That's a 1932 Ford Model A," Jessica explained. "Get it? A deuce is a two, so a '32 is called a Deuce. That's Bruce Sears at the wheel."

"The one whose car had the flat tires?" Frank said.

"Right," Jessica replied.

The speeding roadster made a power slide at the end of the arena and started back along the far side.

"Count on Bruce," Jessica said. "He grandstands even when the stands are empty."

"Look!" Frank exclaimed, pointing. As the hot rod passed them, oily black smoke began to mix with the rooster tail of dust. The car was on fire!

21

3 Feuding Friends

"Fire!" Frank and Joe shouted at the same time.

But the powerful engine of the speeding roadster was making too much noise for them to be heard. Frank watched in horror as Bruce continued to fly around the track, too intent on his driving to be aware of the thickening smoke pouring from under his hot rod. When Bruce came around the second time, Frank waved his arms wildly, trying to attract his attention. Next to him, Joe and Jessica were doing the same. Bruce noticed them, but all he did was grin and wave back.

Jessica exclaimed, "We've got to do something, quick! Where's Keith? Maybe he—"

"I'll stop him," Joe said suddenly. He started

to run into the arena, but Jessica grabbed his arm.

"You'll get yourself killed," she said forcefully. "He's going too fast to stop quickly."

"I guess you're right," Joe said, letting out a frustrated sigh.

Frank looked around frantically. Twenty yards away, next to the bleachers on the arena floor, was an area set off with low sawhorses. Inside the enclosure was a long table and a number of folding chairs. Frank saw something colorful among them that gave him an idea.

He took off at a sprint and leapt the sawhorses like a hurdler. One look under the table and he let out a shout of triumph. There, rolled up in a box, was a bundle of flags—green for go, yellow for caution, checkered black-and-white for the winner . . . and red.

Frank grabbed the red flag and ran out onto the arena floor, waving it.

The Deuce roadster had rounded the far end of the arena and was heading toward Frank. Joe and Jessica still stood at the side of the track, waving their arms. But Bruce continued at high speed.

Frank positioned himself at the very edge of the track and waved the red flag up and down. Out of the corner of his eye, he noticed Jessica next to him, making a motion with her hand across her throat that meant, Shut it down. Bruce *had* to see them and realize that something was wrong.

Finally he slowed down. The red roadster braked to a halt right next to Frank, Joe, and Jessica. Bruce hit the quick release on his safety harness and stood up. The tall blond driver looked annoyed.

"What's going on?" he shouted. "I don't like my practice—"

At that moment, a cloud of dark smoke roiled up from the engine compartment into his face. Choking, he dived over the side of the car, hit the ground, and rolled away.

"Everybody, back off," someone yelled from behind them. "It could blow anytime."

Keith ran up, with Matt and a few others right behind him. All of them were carrying big red fire extinguishers. Frank stepped out of the way as Keith aimed the long black horn of his extinguisher at the engine of the hot rod. He was just pulling out the safety ring when Bruce grabbed his shoulder.

"Oh, no, you don't," he shouted. "You keep your paws off my car."

"It's on fire, you turkey," Keith replied. "We have to put it out."

The three other men holding fire extinguishers paused, wondering what to do. Behind them, a crowd was gathering, drawn by the shouting. Frank noticed one of the spectators, a small man with thinning sandy hair, wearing a short-sleeved khaki bush jacket. He was muttering into a tiny tape recorder.

"Oh, yeah?" Bruce said to Keith. "Look again, yo-yo! Do you see any flames?"

Frank took a quick glance at the car. Bruce was right—there weren't any flames. The smoke seemed to be thinning out rapidly.

"That's oil smoke," Bruce continued. "And I have a pretty good hunch where it came from."

He walked over to the front of the car. Curious, Frank followed him.

Bruce fanned the last of the smoke away and leaned over to look at the engine. "Ha!" he said, straightening up. "That's what I thought. The oil cap is missing. And I'm ready to bet there was an extra quart of oil in the engine, too."

"So as soon as you got moving," said Frank, "the oil spurted out onto the hot engine and started to smoke."

"You got it, buddy," Bruce replied. He spun around and added, "That's right, isn't it, Keith?"

Keith gave him a cold look. "How should I know? It's your heap." He turned away and handed his fire extinguisher to one of the crew members. "Here, Chuck, would you mind putting this back? It looks like we won't be needing it."

Bruce took a couple of steps toward Keith and said loudly, "Disappointed?"

Keith looked at him grimly. "Meaning what, exactly?"

"Maybe this time you figured on doing some real damage," Bruce replied. "Enough to keep

25

me out of the show this weekend. Because we both know the only way you'll ever be as big a star as you pretend is if I'm out of the way."

"Hey, come on, guys," Jessica said, stepping between the two hot-rodders. "You're supposed to be friends, remember?"

Bruce sidestepped her. "What kind of friend tries to ruin my car?" he said, staring at Keith with narrowed eyes.

"What kind of friend makes crazy accusations in front of all these people?" Keith countered.

"I want them to know what kind of snake you are," Bruce said. "And after I finish telling them, maybe I'll rearrange your face for you."

Jessica put her hand on Bruce's arm. "Please," she said. "This isn't solving anything. We've got to work together."

"Not with him, I don't," Bruce replied.

Frank took a step closer to the enraged hot-rodder and said, in a low voice, "There's a short guy to your left who's taping every word you say. Do you want to read about this fight in the next issue of *Motorsports?* It won't help your reputation any."

Bruce frowned at him, then glanced quickly to his left. "Morgan," he muttered. "That guy has a talent for turning up at times like this."

Aloud, he said, "I'm going to let you off the hook this time, Keith, for old times' sake. But if you mess with my car again, you'll end up wearing your head backward."

To Frank and Jessica, Bruce muttered, "It's okay, I'm under control." Then he seemed to take his first good look at Frank. "Hey, listen, who are you?" he added. "Who told you to stick your nose in my business?"

"This is Frank Hardy," Jessica said quickly. "Grant just hired him and his brother, Joe, to help keep the lid on incidents like the one that just happened. It's not going to help our box office if people get the idea that we're always fighting with each other."

Bruce scowled at her. "Ease up, Jess," he said.

"I liked it better when you two were friends," Jessica replied. "What about all the time you spent together when you were partners and had your own hot rod show? Are you just going to forget that?"

"I wish I could," Bruce said. "The show was a flop, remember? We had to fold. That's why we had to take up Grant's offer and join this outfit. We would have been better off if we'd split up for good."

"Bruce, there's one thing I'm wondering about," said Frank. "A minute ago you accused Keith of sabotaging your car. Do you have any proof of that?"

"What's it to you?" Bruce demanded.

"Look," Frank replied. "If I'm going to deal with public relations and questions from reporters, I have to know what's really happening here.

If a question takes me by surprise, I might not be able to handle it well."

Bruce nodded reluctantly. "That makes sense, I guess," he said. "Okay, to answer your question, no, I don't have what you'd call proof, just a strong feeling in my gut. Ever since Keith and I stopped getting along, things have been happening to me. And I don't think they're just coincidence."

"But couldn't Keith say the same thing about you?" Frank pointed out. "He's suffered some pretty questionable accidents lately, too, hasn't he?"

"Those are just smoke screens," Bruce said. "Who'd suspect him of causing the accidents if some of them happen to him?"

"Can you think of anybody else who might want to harm you or the show?" Frank asked.

Bruce shrugged. "Grant's been having a run of good luck lately—bigger bookings, better sales, and now this TV deal. I guess some of the other big car show promoters, people like Bart Preston, may not be too happy about that. But I can't see them sneaking around here to steal my oil cap."

"Hmm," said Frank. "Is there someone inside the show who might have a grudge against either of you?"

Bruce gave him a surprising smile. "Hey," he said, "I'm usually a wonderful guy, everybody's friend. I only get mean when somebody messes with me or my Deuce. Are we done here? I want to get my car backstage and clean off the engine."

He climbed into his car, then called to some of the crew members to give him a push. A few moments later, Frank watched the bright red hot rod roll down the corridor toward the work area. With the central attraction gone, the onlookers drifted away, leaving Frank with Jessica and Joe.

"Hey, I'm sorry, guys," Jessica said, looking at her watch. "I just remembered I'm meeting somebody in five minutes. Will you be okay on your own?"

"I think we can find our way around," Joe replied. "We'll see you later."

"Sure," she said. "See you later." She turned and hurried away.

"Well?" Frank asked Joe. "Did you get anything from Keith?"

"Yeah. He thinks all this is just bad luck. He admits that he and Bruce are on the outs—he says it's because they're always scrambling with each other to be king of the mountain. But he says he's not responsible for any of the accidents."

Frank stared across the empty arena. "What do you think?" he asked.

Joe rubbed the back of his neck. "He wouldn't even listen when I hinted that Bruce might be behind anything."

"I wonder if we're grabbing this case by the wrong end," Frank said. "Some of the incidents could really be just accidents. But we know that extortion note didn't write itself. Maybe we should try concentrating on that angle."

"Good point," Joe said. "Do you think Tucker will lend us the note long enough to take it home and analyze it?"

"Come on," Frank said, heading for the exit. "Let's find him and ask."

The promoter was in his office, poring over a stack of computer printouts. He looked up when Joe and Frank came in. "I hate going over the accounts," he said. "I got into this business because I thought I'd be spending all my time around hot cars and fast bikes. Instead, I'm turning into a paper shuffler. Did you find anything?"

"We're working on it," Frank replied. He explained about wanting to analyze the extortion note.

"Sure, here it is," Tucker said. "I'll get you an envelope."

Joe frowned. "What about the one it came in? That could be important evidence."

Tucker shrugged. "Sorry—I threw it away before I realized what was in it." As Joe and Frank started to go, he added, "I really appreciate your help, guys. I'm counting on you."

Joe and Frank walked back to the main entrance of the arena, where their van was parked. The grass on either side of the walk had just been cut, and a man in work clothes was using a power blower to gather the clippings into a pile. Joe wrinkled his nose at the smell of the exhaust fumes and tried to ignore the racket. He and Frank hurried past and started across the pavement toward the van.

Suddenly a movement caught Joe's attention. He looked around, then urgently pulled Frank back onto the sidewalk. A moment later, a big Harley sped by, close enough for them to feel the breeze of its passage.

"Whew," Frank said. "That was scary. I didn't hear it coming over the racket from that blower."

"You saw who it was, didn't you?" Joe asked. "Fat Dave. Do you think he was trying to hit us?"

Frank shook his head. "Just scare us a little, I think. But did you notice his passenger?"

Joe thought for a moment. "Short and thin, wearing a black helmet with a dark visor, black leather jacket, black jeans. So what?"

"You left out the most important item," Frank said grimly. "Black cowboy boots with white stitching. The same boots Jessica Derey was wearing."

Joe stared at him. "Wait a minute," he said. "We figured that the Skulls might have an inside man who's working with the show. But maybe their inside man is a woman."

"Let's go!" Frank shouted. He set off at a run in the direction of the van. "Maybe we can still catch them."

4 Slippery Surface

Joe ran for the van and yanked open the door on the driver's side. As Frank jumped into the passenger seat, Joe started up the engine. He hit the gas and steered toward the exit of the parking lot. At the street, he paused and looked both ways.

"There they are, at the end of the street," Frank shouted. "They just turned right onto Post Road."

The tires squealed as Joe took off after the vanished motorcycle. "You're sure that was Jessica on the back?" he asked, as they neared the corner. "Maybe it was someone else wearing black cowboy boots."

"Maybe," Frank replied. "I'm sure about see-

32

ing the boots, but I couldn't swear they were exactly the same as Jessica's. I hope not, in a way. I liked her, and I'd hate to think she's involved with Fat Dave."

Joe made the turn and peered up Post Road. Six or eight blocks ahead he saw what looked like the motorcycle. A moment later, it turned left onto a side street. Joe sped up and followed.

"Hey, we're on Buchanan Street," Frank observed. "Isn't that where the Flying Skulls' clubhouse is?"

"I think so," Joe replied.

The motorcycle was increasing its lead, but trying to catch up would have meant taking too many chances, so Joe sat back in his seat and began to take in the scenery as he drove.

They were passing through one of Bayport's older neighborhoods. After a block of stores that included a dry cleaner, a small grocery, and a boarded-up movie theater, they passed block after block of two-story wooden frame houses. Each had a small front yard and a driveway that led back past the side of the house to a one-car garage.

Joe noticed that most of the houses were in good shape, freshly painted, with well-kept yards and window boxes full of flowers. Then he let out a whistle. In the middle of the next block was a house that had to be the Bayport headquarters of the Flying Skulls. It, too, was freshly painted, but in wide stripes of deep blue, bright red, lime

33

green, and fluorescent yellow. Over the door was a wooden sign with a winged skull carved into it. Rows of motorcycles filled the driveway and front yard.

On the porch, a man sat balanced on the back legs of an old wooden chair. He wore a goatee, and his head was totally shaved except for a long ponytail in back. When Joe slowed down to get a closer look at the clubhouse, the man sat up and stared at the van. Frank ducked back to keep his face out of sight, but he knew Fat Dave would be getting a full report about the van before long.

"No sign of Jessica," Joe remarked as he turned the corner at the end of the block.

Frank sighed. "Well, we can't exactly knock on the door and ask if Jessica's there."

"No, I guess not," Joe said. "Oh, well, let's head for home."

Fifteen minutes later, the van pulled into the driveway of the Hardy house and stopped.

"Dad's home," Frank said, pointing to the lighted window of the little study off the living room. "I wonder if he's ever tangled with the Flying Skulls."

"Let's ask him," Joe replied.

Inside the house, the brothers crossed the living room, and Frank tapped on the door of the study. "Busy, Dad?" he asked.

Fenton Hardy, a former New York City policeman, was a well-known private detective. He was always ready to listen to his sons' cases and help them track down important information. Frank and Joe had helped their father out on quite a few cases, too.

Fenton looked up from his typewriter. "Come on in," he said. "I'm nearly finished with this." He continued with his typing for another minute, then sat back and said, "What's up?"

Joe said, "We were wondering if you knew anything about a local motorcycle gang called the Flying Skulls."

"Not very much, I'm afraid," he responded. "Their leader—what's his name, Big Bill?"

"Fat Dave," Frank supplied.

"Right, Fat Dave. He has a pretty shrewd grasp of public relations. What I hear is that the group can be pretty violent, but only when they're sure they won't be tagged for it. As far as I know, they aren't mixed up in anything more criminal than speeding and getting into a lot of brawls. Are they involved in a case of yours?"

"Maybe," Frank said. "They seem to be in a sort of feud with a promoter of hot rod and motorcycle shows named Grant Tucker. He thinks that they're trying to extort money from him."

"Maybe they've gone into a new line of work, then." Mr. Hardy looked thoughtful. "Grant Tucker. Now why does that name sound familiar to me?"

"You've probably seen the commercials for his hot rod show," Joe suggested. "It's opening at the arena tomorrow night."

His father shook his head. "If I did, I didn't pay any attention. No, this goes back two or three years. A story someone told me . . . Oh, yes, of course. A friend of mine who's still on the force had a very frustrating time investigating a complaint against Tucker."

"What sort of complaint?" asked Frank.

"Fraud, basically. Two important investors in Tucker's outfit claimed that the bigger his shows got, the less profit there was for them to share. They accused him of skimming the income from ticket sales. But nothing ever came of it in the end. My friend said he couldn't decide whether Tucker was too clever for him or too honest."

"That's interesting," Joe said. "But I don't see any connection to our case. Not unless those investors decided to hire the Skulls to make trouble for Tucker."

"They'd be better off hiring a good accountant," Fenton said with a smile. "If you like, I'll call a couple of people who might know more about this motorcycle gang."

"Great, Dad," Frank said. "Thanks. If you learn anything important, we'll be in the basement."

The Hardys had converted a small area in the basement to a fingerprint lab and photographic developing studio. For the next hour, Joe and

Frank thoroughly examined the extortion note. Then they sat down at a table and went over their notes together.

"Well," Joe said, "aside from ours, there's only one set of prints on the note. I'm willing to bet they are Tucker's, because it looks like the extortionist left smudges that were probably made by surgical rubber gloves. What about the paper and the cut-out words?"

"It's on ordinary photocopy paper, nothing special at all," Frank said. "But the words are more interesting. About two-thirds of them are cut from the same kind of paper, maybe even from the same piece. And they include the words 'Grant,' 'Tucker,' and 'show,' not to mention the figure '$250,000.' What does that sound like to you?"

Joe was silent for a second. "Wait . . . sure." He snapped his fingers. "An ad for the show. But if the words were cut from an ad, wouldn't we have found printing on the back? I know—they must have come from a leaflet or flyer of some kind."

Frank nodded. "Tomorrow morning, I'll make some enlargements. Then we can check with Tucker about any flyers that match up. It may be a dead end—they must be printed by the thousands—but you never know. Do you notice anything else about the note?"

"It was done by someone with a lot of time and patience," Joe replied. "Look how carefully the words are cut out, and how well they line up. That can't be easy to do wearing rubber gloves."

"Good point," said Frank. "You know what struck me, though? How did Tucker get this note?"

"He said it came this morning. I guess it was in the mail, though he didn't actually say so."

"Um-hum," Frank said, nodding. "And he told us that at first he threw it away. That explains why the page is so crumpled."

"Yeah," Joe said. "So what?"

"The page is loaded with wrinkles," Frank said, "but where are the creases? If it was folded to be put in an envelope, the marks should still show up. But they don't."

Joe took another look at the extortion note, then he said, "Two possibilities I can think of. One, it was mailed flat, in a big envelope. And two—"

Frank completed his thought. "Two, it was never in an envelope at all. Which would mean that Tucker lied to us. Either the note reached him some other way that he wants to conceal for some reason—"

Joe jumped in. "Or he made up the note himself."

When Joe followed Frank into the arena the next morning, he found the preparations for the hot rod show's opening night in full swing. The barnlike work area backstage vibrated with the roars of high-strung engines being tuned. Out on the floor, the stage crew was practicing putting the different pieces of equipment in place, then removing them. This rehearsal was important, Joe knew, because during the actual performance the crew would have to make the scene changes at top speed.

Matt, the crew chief, was limping from place to place, clipboard in hand, taking notes on possible problems. When he noticed Frank and Joe, he nodded.

Bob Morgan, the reporter, appeared from somewhere and came over to the Hardys. "I hear you guys are helping with the press," he said.

"That's right," Frank said cautiously. "We're trainees."

"Oh? Lucky you," Morgan replied. "You'll get a lot of valuable experience here. You take this feud between Keith and Bruce, for instance. It seems to me it's been getting more serious, and these so-called accidents are getting more dangerous. What if somebody gets hurt? How do you plan on handling that?"

Frank looked at the small man and thought that the reporter seemed to have more on his mind than he was revealing.

Morgan grinned. "No comment?" he said slyly. "You'd better start working on one. I suspect you're going to need it. It's funny—Bruce and Keith were such close friends until about a month ago. I wonder what happened?"

Across the way, someone drove a cross-country motorcycle with chromed heavy-duty springs front and rear into the arena and toward the Hardys and Morgan. The rider wore black coveralls and a silver helmet. As the bike drew closer, Frank recognized Jessica. He glanced at her feet, but she was wearing silver boots. Did she also have a black helmet, Frank wondered, like the one he'd seen on Fat Dave's passenger, or had that been someone else?

Jessica slowed down as she approached and called, "Did you guys come to watch me practice?"

"You bet," Morgan called back. "But I thought you always wore a silver jumpsuit with gold zippers."

"Not for practice, silly," Jessica replied. "Come back tonight if you want to see that outfit." She waved, blipped the throttle, and started down the track.

Bob Morgan rubbed his chin and said, "She's got something, Jessica. Maybe her idea of making a pilot for a TV series isn't so dumb. You don't happen to know where the money's coming from, do you? TV production doesn't come cheap."

"Sorry," Frank said. He wished he could ask the reporter a few questions, but he didn't want Morgan figuring out that he and Joe were investigating, too. "No comment," was all Frank said.

"Could the money be coming from Grant?" the reporter continued, turning to Joe. "He's probably got quite a few bucks tucked away somewhere, but I would have thought he'd need them for the show. A really big-time production doesn't come cheap. No, I can't see him putting his nest egg into Jessica's project. Maybe she has a rich aunt."

Joe took note of Morgan but didn't respond. Jessica was approaching on her first circuit. As she passed them, she gunned the engine and brought the front wheel up into the air. Frank wrinkled his nose at the smell of burned rubber. After a wheelie that took her halfway down the track, Jessica bumped the front wheel down, picked up speed, and turned in the direction of the pair of jumping ramps.

"Watch this," Morgan said. "She's good."

Jessica hunched over the handlebars with her weight on the footrests. Frank held his breath. The two ramps looked impossibly steep, high, and far apart. Would she be able to cross the gap between them?

Suddenly, just yards from the takeoff ramp, the speeding motorcycle swerved wildly to the left and went into an uncontrolled skid. Sparks flew as the steel crash bar that guarded the rider's leg scraped along the cement floor under the dirt. At what seemed like the last possible moment, Jessica jumped off the motorcycle. Tucked into a ball, she rolled sideways three times. Then she lay still.

5 Removing the Evidence

Joe, Frank, and Bob Morgan ran across the arena to the fallen motorcyclist. From backstage, others were coming, drawn by the noise of the crash.

One man was carrying a big metal case with a red cross on the side. "Don't let her move," he shouted. "I'm a paramedic."

Joe spotted Jessica's motorcycle lying on its side a few yards away. The engine was still on, spinning the rear wheel at high revolutions. In another moment, the engine might start to burn itself out. Joe started to run toward the cycle, but then he saw Matt hurry to it and turn off the ignition. The arena was abruptly silent.

Joe watched the paramedic check Jessica for major injuries. Then, over his protests, she sat up and took off her helmet. Joe knelt down next to her and tried to help, but she shrugged him off. "I'm okay," she insisted. "It was just a spill. I've taken dozens of worse ones."

"What happened?" Morgan asked. "From where I was standing, it looked as if you decided at the last moment not to try the jump. Why?"

Jessica gave him a sidelong glance and said, "I changed my mind."

The reporter stared at her. "You just changed your mind, like that? You must have been doing fifty miles an hour. You could have been badly hurt!"

From behind him, Grant Tucker said, "Anybody in my show can call off a stunt if it seems like a bad idea."

"That's a good policy," Morgan said, "but it's beside the point. That's not a hard jump for her. She ran a much bigger risk swerving like that than going through with it. I'd like to know why."

"I changed my mind, that's all," Jessica repeated. She looked up at Joe and reached for his hand to pull herself to her feet. As her head neared his, she whispered, "The ramp."

Joe gave her a questioning look.

She nodded very slightly toward the ramp, then said, "I'm going to my dressing room. Bob, why don't you come with me? I can tell you about my plans for my act."

As she and the reporter walked away, followed

by most of the other onlookers, Joe walked over to his brother.

"What's up?" Frank asked.

"Jessica tried to tell me something about the ramp," Joe replied. "Let's take a look."

The floor of the ramp was made of sheet steel with lines of angled ridges for traction. A scaffold of steel pipes supported it. Joe bent down and tried to shake the scaffold. Frank lent a hand, but it didn't budge. When they pushed at the edge of the steel flooring, nothing happened.

"It looks fine to me," Joe said, straightening up. "I don't see—hey, wait!" He had noticed a faint shimmer of pink, green, and blue from the lower surface of the ramp.

"What is it?" asked Frank.

Joe reached down and touched the wet spot with his fingertip. He stood up, rubbed his finger and thumb together, and raised them to his nose to sniff.

"It's oil," he reported. He found a tissue in his back pocket and wiped off his hand. "Jessica must have spotted it as she started toward the ramp. I guess she didn't want to say anything around Morgan."

Frank bent down and felt the surface of the ramp. "You're right," he said. "I wonder . . ."

He walked down the track, then turned around and squatted down until his head was only about three feet from the floor. He walked a few feet toward the ramp, then squatted again.

44

Joe frowned in puzzlement, then grinned. Frank must be trying to get the same perspective that someone riding a motorcycle would have, Joe figured. The idea was great, but it did make him look a little like a duck.

"Well?" Joe asked when his brother returned.

"She must have good eyes," he replied. "I caught a glimpse of the oil from about thirty feet out, but I was looking for it. If I hadn't been, I don't know if I would have noticed anything until I was practically on top of the ramp. And Jessica started her swerve at least fifteen feet away from the ramp, which means she must have spotted it even farther back."

"Unless—" Joe began. An angry voice interrupted him. He turned and saw Bruce Sears, the blond hot-rodder whose car had had oil smoking on its engine the day before.

"What are you two up to, hanging around here?" Bruce was standing a few feet away with a scowl on his face and an orange grease rag in his hand. When he noticed Joe glancing at the rag, he shoved it in the back pocket of his grimy jeans.

"Talking about what happened to Jessica," Frank replied. "She's lucky she wasn't hurt, taking a high-speed spill like that."

Joe decided to see if he could goad Bruce into blowing his cool and maybe making a revealing remark. "Yeah," he said. "And we're all lucky that that Morgan guy wasn't a little closer when it

45

happened. One thing the show doesn't need is bad news."

Bruce gave him a hard stare. "For someone whose job is keeping things quiet," he said, "you talk an awful lot. By the way, I heard Grant asking where you two were, a few minutes ago. Maybe you should go find out what he wants."

Joe felt his face start to turn red, but he kept his temper in check. All he said was, "Thanks for telling us."

As he and Frank walked toward the stage entrance, Joe said, "Why do you suppose he wanted us away from there so badly?"

"Good question," Frank replied. "Let's see if we can find an answer." He took Joe's arm and pulled him behind a metallic green and gold 4x4. Through the truck's rear window, they watched Bruce take the rag from his pocket and wipe off the surface of the ramp, then glance around nervously.

"He knew about the oil," Joe whispered. "Does that mean he put it there?"

"Maybe," whispered Frank. "Look out, he's coming this way."

The Hardys walked around the 4x4, keeping its bulk between themselves and the hot rod driver.

"He's heading for the exit," Joe reported after a cautious peek. "Should we follow him?"

"Let's go," Frank replied.

From the shelter of the exit door, Joe saw Bruce

walk across the parking lot toward a mint-condition muscle car from the 1960s. Its raised rear end and lowered front made it look as if it were speeding downhill, even while it was sitting still.

"Quick, the van," Frank said. "But let's take it at a stroll."

Fighting the impulse to break into a run, Joe walked over to the van, climbed in, and started the engine. Across the way, Bruce was just backing out of his parking space. His car was shaking from side to side from the tremendous power of its huge, souped-up engine.

"Wow," Joe said as Frank climbed into his seat. "Look at that car. Let's face it, if he wants to, he could leave us in the dust."

Ten minutes later, Joe was wishing he hadn't tempted fate. He was driving east on Lafayette Boulevard, approaching the corner of Buchanan Street. Joe had been keeping at least half a block between the van and Bruce's car, but then Bruce slowed down almost to a crawl. Joe came up close behind the muscle car before he noticed that Bruce had come to a complete stop at a traffic light. Then, just as the light changed to yellow, he swerved left onto Buchanan and peeled out, tires smoking.

"He spotted us!" Frank shouted. "Let's move."

Joe caught the last seconds of the yellow light and put the pedal to the floor. The van surged forward. Just then, down the block, a department store delivery truck backed out of a driveway, completely obstructing the street.

Joe shifted his foot to the brake pedal. By the time the street was clear, Bruce and his muscle car were gone.

"Now what?" Joe asked, banging his hands against the steering wheel.

Frank looked around. "Did you notice where we are?" he replied. "About four blocks from the Skulls' clubhouse."

"You think he's Fat Dave's inside man?" Joe asked.

"Let's take a look."

As far as Joe could tell, the motorcycle gang's headquarters looked the same as it had the night before, except that there was a different watchman on the front porch. Bruce's car was nowhere around.

As Joe started back across town, he said, "Either he was going somewhere else, or his business with the Skulls didn't take long."

"There's another possibility," Frank said. "He could have been deliberately luring us away from the arena for some reason. If so, it means that he's somehow penetrated our cover."

"And that he has something to hide," Joe added.

A few minutes later, they returned to the arena. Joe noticed that Bruce's muscle car was parked near the back entrance, in the very spot where the van had been before. And when Joe and Frank walked inside, one of the first people they saw was Bruce. He grinned at them and said, "You been out for a ride?"

"Something like that," Frank said.

"Did I tell you Grant was looking for you?" Bruce continued.

"Yeah, you did," Joe said. "About half an hour ago."

"Well, he's looking for you again," the hot-rodder said. His grin widened. "I'd go get found if I were you."

"Thanks," Joe muttered.

The door to Grant's office was partly open. Frank peeked in. The show promoter was staring down at a computer printout and massaging the back of his neck. When Frank tapped on the door, he looked up.

"Hey, I was just looking for you guys," Tucker said.

"We heard," Frank replied.

"I need a little favor," Grant continued. "I just got a message from Keith Helm. He's stuck out near the expressway with a blown engine. I said I'd send our tow truck over to bring him in, but it turns out I don't have a free driver. You think you guys could handle it? It just means driving the truck over. Keith knows how to operate the lift, and he'd do the driving on the way back."

"Well—" Frank began.

"It'd be a real help," Grant said. "And it'd give

you a chance to ask Keith some more questions about the accidents. What do you say?"

It occurred to Frank that Grant wasn't too clear about whether they were acting as detectives or a car service, but he was right—picking up Keith would be a good way to get to know him better. "Okay," he said, and copied down the directions.

"This is the place," Joe said a few minutes later, as he pulled the tow truck into the driveway of a closed gas station. "But I don't see Keith or his car anywhere. Do you think you took down the wrong address?"

"Uh-oh," Frank said, glancing in the side mirror. "I think we have a problem."

At that moment, a dozen motorcycles swept into the driveway and stopped, surrounding the tow truck.

"What do I do?" Joe asked urgently. "Make a break for it?"

"Too late. We'd better try to talk to them," Frank said. He swung his door open and climbed down. Joe came up beside him.

Five or six of the bikers formed a semicircle around Frank and Joe. One of them, shirtless under a leather vest, held a heavy wrench in his right hand and bounced the head of it in the palm of his other hand. Another guy was pulling on a pair of black gloves with pyramid-shaped metal studs along the knuckles.

"Hi, guys," Frank said. "How's it going?"

The man with the goatee and shaved head,

who had been on guard duty the day before, stepped forward. "We want you to take a message to Tucker," he said. "Here it is: We'll be at the show tonight, but he'd better not think he can buy us for a few free passes. Tell him we'll let him know what we want, and tell him he'd better come through with it. We don't play around."

"Sure," Frank said. "We'll be glad to give him your message."

"That's just the words part," the biker said. "Here's the rest."

He gave a nod, and two guys jumped Frank. He started to struggle, then stopped. There wasn't much he could do against two armlocks and a choke hold.

Next to him, Joe also had been jumped. "Hey!" Joe shouted. "Let me go!" Then he, too, was immobilized.

"Tell Tucker we gave you a free sample," the guy with the goatee said. "Harry?"

The biker with the wrench gave Frank a gap-toothed smile, raised the tool over his head, and took a step toward him.

6 Flyaway Wheel

The biker stepped closer to Frank. He held the heavy wrench above Frank's head. Taking a deep breath, Frank let it out slowly and deliberately relaxed the muscles of his shoulders and upper arms. His best chance—maybe his only chance —was to fool the two who were holding him into letting down their guard, if only for a moment.

He visualized a ball of energy gathering in his middle, tightening and tightening, ready to explode outward. But just as he was about to drive his elbows into the stomachs of his two attackers, the biker with the wrench turned slightly to the left and walked past him and Joe.

Frank's puzzlement turned to anger as the biker swung the wrench full force against the side window of the tow truck. Tiny particles of safety glass showered the parking lot and glittered blue-green in the sunlight. Moving to the other side of the truck, the biker shattered a second window, then stepped back with a satisfied smile.

"Like I said," the one with the shaved head growled, "just a little sample. Tell Tucker that next time it could be somebody's face. Okay, boys, let them go."

Frank shook his arms free and rubbed his aching elbows. Next to him, Joe seemed to be memorizing the faces of the two bikers who had been holding him. Around them, motorcycle engines coughed and sputtered into life. The rumble rose to a shriek as the twelve bikers raced their engines triumphantly. At a nod from the leader, they made a jackrabbit start and swept under the gas station canopy before curving back to pass Frank and Joe on the way to the street.

Frank stared after them, his fists clenched. In his mind he still saw the nasty grin the leader had given them as the band sped past. He was sure he wouldn't forget that look for a long time.

"Well," Joe said. "How can we arrange a rematch, with a little better odds?"

"I'll be working on it," Frank promised. "Right now, we'd better get back to the arena. I'd like a few words with one or two people, Keith for a start. Someone told the Skulls where to find us, and I'm going to find out who."

Joe found a hammer in the truck's toolbox and used the handle to knock out the remaining shards of the two shattered windows. Frank swept the tiny pieces of glass off the passenger seat and the floor. Then Joe got the tow truck started and headed back to the arena.

"You think it was Keith who set us up?" Joe asked.

"We'll see," Frank replied in a grim voice. "Somebody did, that's for sure."

"Which means that same somebody must know who we are and what we're really doing at the show."

Frank hesitated, then said, "Maybe. But maybe not. Remember, the Skulls didn't threaten us specifically. Nobody said, 'Give up the case or else.' It was as if they didn't even care who we were, just as long as we worked for Tucker."

Joe slowed down and turned into the arena parking lot. A glossy maroon low-slung fifties vintage convertible with three chrome air cleaners sticking up through the hood swooped past and turned in ahead of the van.

"That was Keith!" Joe exclaimed. He downshifted and hit the gas. The rear tires gave a squeal of protest as the heavy vehicle shot forward.

"Easy," Frank warned. "He's not going far. If we don't catch him in the parking lot, we can always find him inside."

Frank spotted the convertible. Keith was just

putting up the power top, which jutted up into the air like a sail. Joe pulled into a nearby space, and he and Frank got out.

"No point in locking the truck," Joe muttered as they walked toward Keith's car. "Not with two windows out."

Keith turned around as Frank and Joe drew closer, giving Frank a chance to admire his Hawaiian shirt. On the front of it was a brightly colored parrot.

"Hey there," Keith said. "You fellows settling in okay?"

"Yes and no," said Frank. "How's your engine trouble?"

Keith wrinkled his forehead. "Me?" he said. "Why do you think I've got engine trouble?"

Joe said, "Grant got a message that you were across town with a blown engine. We just took the tow truck out to pick you up."

"It must have been somebody's idea of a joke," Keith said with a shrug. "I went off to get a hamburger, that's all."

"Did you tell anybody you were leaving?" Frank asked, trying to sound casual.

Keith eyed him curiously. "Well," he said slowly, "sure I did. I told Matt we could work on my dragster when I got back. And I asked Grant for an appointment for this afternoon. A few months ago I would have just walked over and started talking, but these days we ask for appointments."

"Is that it?" Joe asked. "Just Matt and Grant?"

"No. I asked Jessica if she wanted anything from the burger joint. And anybody standing around could have overheard. Listen, what is all this, anyway?"

"When we got to the place where you supposedly broke down," said Frank, "a bunch of bikers jumped us. They said they had a message for Grant. Then they smashed two of the windows on the tow truck."

Keith rolled his eyes. "I knew we were heading for trouble," he said. "I told Grant not to get mixed up with that gang, but he's too much of a biker himself to listen. Come with me, you guys. I want you to tell him what happened to you. He'd better cut some kind of deal with the Skulls, that's all. It isn't just his show he's risking with this feud, it's all of our careers."

Grant Tucker was inside the work area, talking to Bob Morgan. As Frank approached, he heard Grant say, "The field is wide open. Not a day goes by that I don't think of another possible tie-in." Then he noticed Frank, Joe, and Keith and said, "Good, you got back. How bad is your engine, Keith?"

"It's fine," Keith replied. "That's not the trouble."

"Trouble?" Grant repeated, raising his eyebrows. He looked at Frank, who nodded slightly, then glanced over at Bob Morgan. Grant caught the unspoken message. "Uh, Bob," he said, "I'd love to tell you more about my ideas, but we're opening in a few hours, and I—"

"Hey, no problem," the reporter said. "I'll catch you at a better time." He nodded to Keith and the Hardys and walked away.

Keith waited until Morgan was out of hearing range, then told Grant what had just happened to Joe and Frank. "I don't know what you told these guys about their jobs," he concluded, "but I bet it didn't include being roughed up by the Flying Skulls."

"They didn't really rough us up," Joe said.

"Wait till next time," Keith replied. "Come on, Grant. You've got to see that it's time to quit stalling and settle with Fat Dave. There's a lot riding on this show."

"You don't have to tell me that," the promoter said. "And I'm on top of the situation. The Skulls won't bother us much longer. Now, I really do have a lot to take care of before showtime."

"So do I, man," Keith said. "I'm one of your stars, remember?"

As Keith left, Joe said, "I'd better go pull the tow truck inside. With those windows out, somebody might decide to help himself to the radio."

"Sure, thanks," Grant called as Joe started toward the parking lot. "I appreciate it. And I'm sorry about what you two just went through."

Frank stayed behind. "I'm going to look around

a little," he told Grant. "By the way, I've got a question about the message that was supposed to be from Keith—how did you get it?"

"Sally, the receptionist, must have taken the call. I found the message slip on my desk," Grant replied. "That was about five minutes before I sent you and Joe out. Listen, I am sorry about what happened. I had no way of knowing—"

"That's okay," Frank said quickly. "But do you mind if I ask Sally about the phone call? Maybe she recognized the voice."

"Sure, go ahead," Grant said. "Let me know what you find out." He walked off before Frank could reply.

Frank went upstairs to the offices and found the receptionist at her desk. She couldn't help him much.

"Yes, I took the call," she told him. "It was a man's voice, but I can't say whose. I don't really know the people in this company. I work for the arena, not for the hot rod show."

"Okay, thanks," Frank replied, and made his way back to the work area. It was time to take a more careful look around.

The work area was filled with deafening noise and the choking fumes of burning gasoline, methanol, and the castor oil lubricant used in racing engines. He hurried through. On the other side of a sliding door was an unlit garage area where the vehicles not being worked on were kept.

Nearest the door was Bigfoot. In the shadowy light, the huge 4x4 looked like a prehistoric monster. Frank stepped up next to it. He stood six-foot-one, but he could barely reach the top of one of the immense tires, designed for earth-moving equipment. He shook his head in amazement and walked on.

The line of cars seemed endless. Just behind Bigfoot was a souped-up 4x4 pickup. It was black with an orange-flame paint job and twin chrome exhaust pipes that ran up along the back edge of the cab. After that came what looked like an ordinary coupe. But upon closer inspection, Frank noticed the superwide rear tires and the four oversize tailpipes.

As he was looking over the cars, Frank heard a faint noise somewhere farther into the garage. He peered through the semidarkness and wished he had his powerful flashlight, which was under the driver's seat of his van.

About fifty feet away, the rectangle of a doorway appeared for a moment, then vanished. Frank set off at a run. Finding the door seemed to take forever, but at last he shoved it open and dashed through.

"Hey, not so fast, you," someone said loudly, grabbing his arm. It was Bruce.

"Did you see someone come through this door just now?" Frank demanded, pulling his arm away.

"Yeah, I did," Bruce replied, stepping in front of him and blocking his way. "And I'd like to know what you were doing in the garage."

"I was looking over the cars," Frank said. "And I startled somebody who was hiding in there. He ran through this door. You didn't see him?"

Bruce shook his head. "I didn't see anybody but you. And with everything that's been happening, it's not a great idea to go hanging around the cars. You understand, buddy? Watch your step."

After dinner, Frank and Joe returned to the arena for the opening of the Tucker show. Frank was amazed at the way the hectic confusion backstage cleared up just in time for the opening parade of trucks, cars, and motorcycles. He and Joe followed the tail of the procession through the tunnel to the arena floor.

They stood next to the stage entrance to watch as the parade continued. It circled the arena, then returned to the stage entrance. Frank and Joe pressed themselves against the wall as Bigfoot, bringing up the rear, came by. The huge 4x4 looked as if its cab roof was going to hit the top of the tall archway that led backstage.

Frank nudged Joe and pointed across the arena. The Flying Skulls, in their reserved section of seats, were shouting back and forth to one another, stomping on the wooden bleachers, and yelling for the show to begin.

At that moment, a team of motorcyclists entered the arena and began a series of precision maneuvers that brought them within inches of crashing into one another. The Skulls stood on their seats and whistled and yelled so loudly that the team lost its concentration and almost messed up an intricate double figure eight. Frank met Joe's eye and made a disgusted face.

The next event was a duel between Bruce, in his Deuce roadster, and Keith, in a dragster. Its driving seat hung a couple of feet back behind the rear wheels. The audience sat up taller as the two cars were rolled to the starting line and the drivers fired up their engines. Frank clapped his hands over his ears as the starter held up his flag and the drivers revved their engines.

The flag dropped. Both cars came off the starting line with their rear wheels smoking and their noses in the air. Sparks flew from the antiflip bars welded to their rear axles. Frank held his breath. The cars were a third of the way down the length of the arena, still doing wheel stands. Suddenly the shouts from the audience changed to screams. The left front wheel of the Deuce came loose and went flying across the arena like a giant Frisbee.

7 Stakeout

Joe grabbed Frank's arm and shouted, "He's going to crash!" In the stands, the spectators jumped to their feet, shouting out in fear. Bruce's flyaway wheel sailed through the air. When it hit the ground, it bounced high and slammed into the chain-link fence protecting the audience.

Bruce brought his remaining front wheel onto the pavement and began to pump the brakes. But Joe knew he couldn't keep balanced much longer. Once the car slowed down enough, the front end would dip and the brake drum would hit the ground. Then the car might start doing cartwheels across the floor.

Joe let go of Frank's arm and started to run out

into the arena, but Frank held him back. He watched as the Deuce roadster suddenly swerved to the left and pointed its radiator straight at the low cement wall surrounding the arena. There was a gasp from the audience. But a moment later, the car was sliding sideways, still upright and quickly losing speed. The smell of burning rubber filled the huge enclosed stadium.

Then, almost without warning, the crisis was over. Joe let out a sigh of relief as the candy-red hot rod slid to a halt just a few feet from the concrete barrier. Its left front end settled quietly onto the exposed brake drum. The crowd, still on their feet, started to cheer wildly.

Half a dozen crew members rushed past Joe and Frank and ran to help Bruce, but he pushed them away. Taking off his helmet, he stood up on the seat of his crippled car and waved to the cheering crowd. Then he walked slowly, still waving, toward the exit.

"That could have been a really bad accident," Joe said to Frank.

"You're right," Frank replied. "But I wonder if it was an accident."

Bruce was walking toward them on his way offstage. As he drew closer, he noticed Frank and Joe. His expression was not friendly.

Joe glanced away and saw that Keith, Bruce's rival in the duel, had apparently missed the whole incident. Once his slingshot dragster crossed the finish line and got the checkered flag, he shut down, braked to a stop, and looked around. He seemed puzzled to find that no one was paying attention to him. Finally one of the crew went over and spoke to him. He too climbed out and walked toward the exit.

As Bruce neared the stage entrance, Grant ran up to him. "That was a great piece of driving," he said, slapping him on the back. "Really fantastic! I just wish we had caught it on film."

Bruce's face reddened. "I came this close to breaking my neck"—he held his two fingers apart slightly—"and all you care about is taking pictures of it? Get lost, Tucker!"

"Now hold on," the show promoter began.

Bruce pushed by him and strode over to face Frank. "I ought to grind you to a powder," he said through gritted teeth. "And if you're not out of here in five minutes, I will!"

"Hey, what's your problem?" Joe demanded.

Bruce waved his finger in Frank's face and said, "This creep messed with my car and nearly got me killed. You think that wheel came off by accident? No way!"

Frank started to answer Bruce, but Grant Tucker stepped in front of the angry hot-rodder. "Hang loose, Bruce," he said. "Something broke, that's all. What do you expect? That Model A of yours is almost old enough to collect Social Security."

"I put in a new front end less than a year ago," Bruce replied. "Those wheel lugs didn't break, somebody loosened them. And I'm betting that this is the jerk who did it."

Once more he pointed at Frank, adding, "I saw him sneaking out of the garage just a couple of hours ago."

Frank hesitated before he responded. He would blow his and Joe's cover if he admitted that he'd been looking for the person who was causing the accidents. But if he didn't answer Bruce's accusation, it would seem like a confession of guilt.

A little circle of crew members and performers had formed around the Hardys. The circle began to close in on them, and Frank sensed that the mood was turning ugly.

"Now hold on," Frank said loudly to Bruce. "Sure, I was in the garage this afternoon. And I saw someone doing something to one of the cars. I couldn't tell which one. And when I tried to chase him, you stopped me."

At that moment, Keith pushed through the crowd. "What's the idea? We've got a show to do."

"The show can wait. I just caught the guy who's been causing the accidents," Bruce replied.

Keith stared at him. "You mean Frank? You've got oatmeal for brains, Bruce. He and Joe have only been with the show for two days, and we've been having funny accidents for a couple of weeks."

Bruce wheeled around, fists raised. "You call it funny when I lose a front wheel halfway down the strip?"

Grant put one big hand on Bruce's chest and the other on Keith's. "That's enough," he growled, shoving them apart. "You guys can continue this on your own time. Matt? Get those cars offstage, pronto. We've got to set up for the tug of war. The customers are starting to get impatient."

Frank glanced behind him, into the arena. Grant was right. Led by the group of bikers, the spectators were beginning to stamp their feet in unison. They were cheering wildly for the show to continue.

A low rumble came from backstage. Frank turned around to see what was happening.

"Make way, there—coming through!" someone shouted.

Frank and Joe pressed themselves against the wall of the tunnel as two big 4x4 pickups, one maroon, the other gleaming black, edged through the crowd of crew members. Both trucks had thick, heavily braced chrome roll bars mounted behind their cabs. Rows of powerful off-road headlights were attached to the cab roofs, and both front bumpers sported heavy-duty power winches. Frank smiled and wondered what use any of the accessories would be inside the Bayport Arena.

A third pickup followed them, with a thick logging chain piled in the back. Frank, Joe, and the others went out to watch.

The two competitors took their positions, back-to-back, in the center of the arena. Crew members set up three evenly spaced white barriers between them, then fastened the ends of the logging chain to their tow bars. The two powerful trucks crept forward, in opposite directions, until the chain was taut between them. Then the starter tied a bright red handkerchief to the chain, exactly over the middle barrier, and stepped back.

Grabbing a microphone that was lowered from the ceiling, the starter said, "Ladies and gentlemen, you're about to witness a battle of titans. These two four-bys are perfectly matched, so what we're going to see is really a test of driving skill. The first stump-puller who manages to get the handkerchief past the barrier on his side is the winner. Drivers, are you ready?"

The engines roared as he raised the green flag, then dropped it. Frank watched, fascinated. For the first minute or two, nothing at all seemed to happen. The two trucks simply sat in the same spots where they had started. Only the vibration of the chain that joined them showed the horsepower being pitted against each truck.

Suddenly, the tires on the maroon 4x4 started

to spin. Black smoke poured up from under its fenders. For a moment, the handkerchief seemed to move in the direction of the spinning truck. Then the better traction of the black truck took over. Slowly the handkerchief crept off center. As it inched toward the winner's line, the crowd roared.

Frank caught Joe's eye and motioned with his head toward backstage. They walked through the tunnel, then found a door at the far end that led to the dressing rooms.

"Whew," Joe said. "That's better. I couldn't even hear myself think out there. That crowd's getting out of hand. Are we heading anywhere in particular, or just looking for some quiet?"

Frank was studying his program. "According to this," he replied, "Jessica Derey's act doesn't go on until nearly the end of the show. I wonder if she'd talk to us now."

Joe shrugged. "It can't hurt to try."

Frank spotted the stunt cyclist's dressing room near the end of the corridor and tapped on the door.

"Come on in," she called. "It's open." When she saw Joe and Frank, she added, "Oh, it's you guys. How do you like the show so far?"

"I'm worried," Frank said. "You heard what happened to Bruce?"

Jessica nodded and said, "I saw it."

"Did you hear that he accused me of loosening his wheel?" Frank continued. "I don't know why.

68

And then I remembered what happened to you this afternoon. I was around then, too. You can see why I'm worried."

Jessica ran her fingers through her hair and said, "They can't think you put that oil on the ramp. You guys were clear across the track, talking to Bob Morgan, weren't you?"

"Yes, we were," Frank replied. "But it looks to me as if the only way I can clear myself is to find out who really is behind these incidents. And I wanted to ask you to help."

Out of the corner of his eye, he noticed a startled glance from Joe. He ignored it and kept his gaze focused on Jessica. She looked troubled.

"Well . . . sure," she finally said. "We can't put on a good show if we're always watching our backs, can we? And Saturday's show is super important, because of the network TV coverage. But what can I do? I'm no detective."

"You can tell us about the people in the company," Frank replied. "You know them, and we don't."

She frowned. "But why?" she demanded. "I can't believe anybody in the company is behind all this. We're like a family."

"Some pretty ugly things can happen inside families," Joe pointed out.

"Yes, but—" She picked up her watch from the dressing table and looked at it. "Listen, guys," she said. "I'm sorry, but I've got to get ready for my act. Why don't we talk tomorrow?"

Frank studied her face. There didn't seem to be any point in arguing. "Fine," he said, and led Joe out of the dressing room.

For the rest of the evening, Joe and Frank roamed around the backstage area, getting to know people's faces and jobs and watching for anything out of the ordinary. Joe kept glancing over his shoulder, expecting another emergency, but nothing happened. As Bigfoot began its noisy trip over the tops of a dozen parked cars for the grand finale, he felt almost let down. Then he had an idea.

"I think we should stay here tonight," he told Frank. "Maybe we can trap the person who's causing the accidents. Let's go find Grant and clear it with him."

The Hardys found Grant Tucker, a smile on his face, standing near the officials' booth.

"So far, so good," he said when Joe and Frank came over. "Except for Bruce's problem, of course. He was right, by the way. The lug bolts on that wheel didn't break—they were unscrewed."

"Pretty dangerous for a practical joke," Joe observed. To himself, he wondered why Grant didn't seem more upset about the sabotage.

"Hmmm?" the promoter replied. "Oh—yeah. But I have a lot of confidence in you guys. One thing I am a little worried about, though, is the crowds. The Skulls whipped the audience into a frenzy tonight. That can't happen Saturday, with the live coverage—the announcers won't be heard over the noise of the crowd."

"They were getting a bit out of control," Joe agreed. He glanced around, to see if anybody could overhear, then continued. "We were thinking we should hang around tonight, in case our bad guy tries any more dirty tricks."

"Whatever it takes," Grant said. "Do you want me to say a word to the guards?"

"No, don't tell anyone," Joe said quickly. "But it might be handy to have a note from you, authorizing us to be here, just in case."

Two hours later, Joe and Frank were sitting hunched down in the cab of a 4x4, looking out into the darkened garage. The last crew member had left, and only the occasional rounds of the watchman had broken the silence since. Joe was thinking hard about the tickling sensation in his nose, wondering if he was about to sneeze, when he felt Frank's hand on his arm.

At the far end of the garage, the dark gray rectangle of an opened door had just appeared. Joe strained his ears and thought he heard slow footsteps. A dim beam of light began to wander through the ranks of parked cars, pausing now and then. Joe eased his door open, glad that the tape he had put over the switch kept the ceiling light from coming on and betraying him.

Once he was out of the truck, Joe gripped the flashlight with his thumb on the switch, ready to turn it on. He sensed that Frank was already tracking the intruder.

The dimmed light had just stopped next to a dragster. Joe wondered if it was Keith's. Circling around to the rear, Joe took a deep breath and waited for Frank to give the signal. A moment later, Joe heard his brother's voice say, "Okay, hold it right there."

Joe hit the button on his light. The brightness of the beam dazzled his dark-adapted eyes, but he could still see the figure next to the dragster straighten up and lurch in Frank's direction. In the man's hand was a heavy crowbar, raised to strike.

8 A Nasty Joke

The menacing figure pulled back his arm, then threw the iron bar in Frank's direction. At the same time, Frank crouched down, his reflexes responding on cue. The bar missed him by inches. An instant later there was a loud *clang*. The crowbar slammed against the fender of the car next to Frank and fell to the floor.

Frank dodged behind his attacker and grabbed him around the chest and upper arms. His captive stamped on Frank's foot and almost twisted free, but Frank managed to hold on until Joe reached him and grabbed the man's arm.

Joe shone his light on their captive's face. It was Matt, the crew chief.

"So you're the one," Frank said, facing him.

"Whose wheel were you planning to loosen this time?"

"What are you talking about?" Matt replied, panting. "I came back to look around. I was afraid somebody might be messing with the cars. And what did I find? You guys. It looks like Bruce was right about you. Wait till I tell Grant what kind of creeps he just hired."

Frank studied Matt's face. He looked angry and upset, but at what? At them, because he really believed they were the bad guys? Or at being caught when he himself was about to sabotage another car?

"We weren't doing anything to the cars," Frank said. "We were waiting to see if anybody else tried to. And then you turned up."

"I don't believe you," Matt replied. "And I don't think anybody else will, either. You guys will be lucky if you get away from the show in one piece."

Joe bent down and picked up the crowbar. Matt flinched as Joe held the long iron bar near his face. "Do you always carry your tools with you?" Joe asked. "Or only when you're planning to use them on somebody's car?"

"Hey, I was coming here alone," the crew chief said. "I didn't know who or what I'd find. I thought I might need some protection."

"Somebody's coming," Frank said suddenly. "Joe, kill the light." He grabbed Matt's arm and pulled him toward the shelter of a nearby 4x4. For a moment, Matt resisted. Then, as the door at the far end of the garage opened, he followed quietly.

The newcomer was carrying a powerful flashlight in one hand and a plastic bag in the other. He walked straight to a slingshot dragster that Frank recognized as Keith's. Resting his flashlight on the car, he began to do something to the exposed engine. When he leaned forward into the light, Frank recognized the tall man with blond hair. It was Bruce.

Frank tapped on Joe's arm and pointed to the left. Then Frank crept around to the right. He sensed that Matt was right in back of him. Bruce was too involved in what he was doing to hear them creep up on him. Then Matt's foot bumped into something that clattered and rolled away.

Bruce spun around. "Who's there?" he demanded.

Frank and Joe switched on their flashlights. "Some witnesses," Frank said.

"You guys!" Bruce exclaimed. "What are you doing here?"

"Waiting to trap someone sabotaging the cars," Joe said. "And now we've got our man."

"Me? You've got the wrong guy," Bruce said.

"Oh, come on," Frank said. "Why deny it? We watched you doing something to Keith's engine."

"That was just for a laugh," the hot-rodder

replied. "Besides, what if I say you're lying? Who in the show is going to take your word against mine?"

Matt stepped into the light. "Me, for one," he announced. "I saw you, too. And I want to know what you did to that engine."

The crew chief limped over to the dragster and bent down to look at the engine. A few moments later, he made a disgusted noise and straightened up. In his hand was a cardboard tube about four inches long, covered with red paper. Two wires protruded from one end.

"A car bomb," he announced. "Some joke, Bruce. I wonder how many people will laugh."

Bruce turned pale. "Hey, there's nothing dangerous about it," he insisted. "All it does is whistle and let off smoke. I just wanted to tease Keith a little."

Frank took the red cylinder from Matt and read the label. "Well, this seems to be what you say it is," he said. "But after everything that's been going on, don't you think this is a bad time to be playing practical jokes on people?"

Bruce seemed to be getting over the shock of being caught. "It's none of your business what I do," he said with a scowl. "Don't forget, in this show I'm a big star and you're a bunch of nobodies. One word from me, and you're out on your ears."

Matt stepped forward and waved his fist in

76

Bruce's face. "I ought to flatten you for that," he said. "I was headlining Tucker's shows before you knew enough to tell a piston from a can of beans."

"I didn't mean you, Matt," Bruce said quickly, taking a step backward. "I've got a lot of respect for you, you know that. I was talking about these two snoops. They don't belong with the show, and I'm going to tell Grant so, first thing tomorrow morning."

"Don't forget to tell him how you tried to wire fireworks to Keith's engine," Frank said.

"But if you do forget," Joe added, "we'll see to it that he knows."

"And I'll see to it that Keith knows," Matt said. "He's not going to be very happy about it."

"I couldn't care less," Bruce said. "I'm getting out of here, and you'd better not try to stop me."

Joe swept his arm out in a mocking gesture and said, "Be our guest."

As Bruce walked toward the door at the far end of the garage, Matt turned his flash toward Frank and Joe. "I'd still like to know what you guys were really doing here tonight," he said.

"That's funny," Frank replied. "I was just thinking the same thing about you."

The next morning, Frank and Joe found Grant in his office and told him what had happened. Tucker paced over to the window, then back to his desk.

"Bruce, huh?" he said. "I never saw him as a practical joker. What do you think?"

Frank frowned thoughtfully. "It's a pretty nasty kind of joke, when you consider everything that's been happening. But I don't think it would have been dangerous. Though, at the moment, I can't see how it fits in with everything else, such as the extortion note. We'll have to keep working on it."

Frank pulled a small stack of enlargements from a manila envelope. "We took a close look at the note, and a lot of the words look as if they were cut out of a flyer for your show." He spread the photos out on the desk and pointed. "Does any of it look familiar?"

The promoter scratched behind his ear as he studied the enlargements. "We circulate a lot of publicity, and we don't save copies of everything. But I have a feeling— Got it! About a year ago, we were performing at a state fairground out west. Old Home Week or something. The locals sponsored a motocross competition as part of the event and put up a quarter-million worth of prizes."

Frank watched Tucker cross to the file cabinet. After a few moments of searching through the drawers, he came back with a leaflet in his hand. "Here we go," he said. "What do you think?"

As Joe arranged the enlarged words from the extortion note next to the flyer, Frank felt a growing sense of excitement. He compared the two, then said, "No doubt about it, if you ask me." He pointed to the word "Tucker." "Look at the way the *k* is tilted a little to the left."

"And that tiny white spot in one of the zeros," Joe added. "But do you see what this means? The extortionist must have had one of these leaflets to cut up for the note. So he must have been with the company last year, when this show took place, or at least been in the same area at the time."

"Well, no," Grant said, with reluctance in his voice. "Not necessarily. We don't always use up all the leaflets we print for a particular show. If we've got a few thousand left over, we hang on to them and use them for scratch paper. Here, look." He reached across the desk and grabbed the top sheet of a stack of paper. "This is from about six weeks ago, and you can see how thick the stack is."

"Still," said Frank, "someone who was around a year ago would be more likely to have this leaflet. Can you give us a list of people who've been with the show that long?"

"That's going to be just about everybody," Grant said unhappily. "And this is a pretty big outfit. I'll have to go through a lot of records. Listen, I'll try to have a list for you sometime this afternoon, but no promises. Every time I turn around, I've got twenty more things to do."

"Sorry," Frank said. "Oh, by the way—that extortion note. How did you get it? By mail? Did you save the envelope?"

"No, I tossed it," Grant replied. "As for whether it came in the mail, I don't really remember. All I remember is finding it on my desk, reading it, and throwing it away. Then later, when I decided to call you guys, I had to go hunt for it in the wastebasket. Why? Is it important?"

Frank said, "It might be. If you remember any more details, let us know. We'll see you later."

As he followed Frank downstairs and into the work area, Joe said, "His memory seems to have a few holes in it."

"I noticed," Frank replied. "What I'd like to know is whether the holes mean anything. He's a busy guy, but you'd think he'd try to be more helpful."

"Uh-oh. I have a feeling we're about to have some trouble," Joe said.

Frank looked in the direction of Joe's gaze. Up ahead, Keith and one of the mechanics were squatting down, looking at the front suspension of a fifties vintage hot rod. Bruce was walking toward them with an open can of motor oil in his hand and a look on his face like that of a little boy who's about to pull a dirty trick. Just as he came even with Keith, Bruce stepped on a socket wrench and seemed to lose his balance. A moment later, a stream of oil poured down onto the back of Keith's T-shirt.

Keith gave a shout and jumped up, pulling the oil-soaked shirt off. Joe was getting ready to jump in and help break up the approaching fight when Frank nudged him and whispered, "Look at Keith's shoulder."

Joe looked, then raised his eyebrows in surprise. The tattoo at the top of Keith's left arm was faint but unmistakable. It was a skull with wings on each side, the emblem of the Flying Skulls.

9 Blown Cover

"Do you think Keith's a member of the Skulls?" Joe whispered to Frank.

"That tattoo has to mean something," Frank replied. "And if what we're thinking is true, it would explain a lot of what's been happening. Come on, we'd better keep these guys apart."

As they moved closer, Joe saw a grin on Bruce's face as he said, "Sorry, fella. I tripped."

Breathing hard, Keith wadded up the oil-soaked T-shirt and flung it in his rival's face. "Sorry, buddy," he said. "It slipped out of my hand."

Several mechanics formed a circle around the two. It seemed to Joe that they were more interested in watching a fight than in stopping one.

Bruce dropped the T-shirt on the cement floor and wiped his face. Then, with no warning, he sprang at Keith, hands outstretched, reaching for his throat.

Keith dodged to the left and brought up his right arm. The elbow caught Bruce under the chin. He staggered backward, clutching his throat. As Keith started to lunge, Joe jumped in front of him. Two men in mechanics' overalls were holding Bruce.

"What's going on here?" Grant pushed his way through the onlookers. Standing with hands on hips, he glared first at Keith, then at Bruce. "I've had all of this feuding that I'm going to take," he said in an angry voice.

Keith sidestepped Joe and pointed at Bruce. "He—" he began.

"I don't care who did what," Grant said, interrupting him. "Any more fights and I'm docking both of you. Got it?" He looked around the little circle. "And what about the rest of you? Don't you have anything to do but stand around? We have a big show tonight, remember?"

Slowly the crowd began to break up, until only Joe, Frank, and the two rivals were left.

Grant turned back to Bruce and Keith. "You're both a mess," he said. "Go get cleaned up. And this is the last time I'll say it—no more fights!"

Bruce and Keith stalked away toward the door. Grant watched them go, then turned back to Joe and Frank. "Would you believe that those guys were best friends when they joined the show a few months ago?" he said. "I guess when their own outfit went under, it put a lot of strain on them."

"What happened?" Joe asked.

"With their show? The usual story. Not enough money socked away to carry them through a dry spell. There's still room for small outfits, but only if they have some money behind them. Bruce and Keith didn't."

"I wonder how they feel about working for someone else instead of themselves," Frank said.

"Hmmph," Grant replied. "If they've got any sense, they're glad to have somebody else take care of the business end. I wish I did."

"Speaking of money," Frank said, "tonight's supposed to be the deadline for the payoff. If we have to go through with it, will you be able to have the money ready?"

"A quarter of a million bucks?" Grant said, rolling his eyes. "In cash?" He glanced around, then lowered his voice to add, "Yeah, I've already got it. But if you fellows don't manage to get it back somehow, it's goodbye to the Tucker Hot Rod, 4x4, and Motorcycle Show."

"We'll do our best," Joe promised.

"Sure you will," Grant muttered. "I just hope your best is good enough."

"So do I," Joe confided to Frank, as the promoter walked away. "I don't feel like we have a grip on this case yet."

"We're starting to," Frank replied. "But we've got to go on the offensive. Let's go out to the van, where no one can overhear us, and plan some strategy."

As they reached the door, Joe saw Bob Morgan coming in. The thin, short man stopped them and said, "I was just coming to look for you. What's the story with Bruce Sears losing that front wheel last night?"

"Weren't you there?" Joe asked. "If you were, you must have seen what happened."

"Is it true that someone loosened the lug bolts to cause the accident?" the reporter pressed.

"Let's put it this way," Frank said. "The bolts didn't break off, so they must have come loose. *How* they came loose, nobody knows."

"Bruce accused you of doing it, didn't he?" Morgan asked.

"He was overexcited," Frank replied. "He didn't know what he was saying."

"What about later last night?" Morgan continued. "I hear that somebody who is a very important part of the show was found booby-trapping somebody else's car. Can you comment on that?"

"Nope," Joe said briskly. "No comment."

The reporter persisted. "I also hear that the show is suffering a very serious cash drain and may not be able to stay in business. Any comment?"

"You'll have to ask Grant about that," Frank

said. "But if I were you, I wouldn't be standing too close to him when I did it."

Morgan smiled. "In my line of work, I've had to get good at ducking," he said. "Thanks for all your help."

As they walked toward the van, Joe said in a low voice, "Why did he thank us? We didn't tell him anything, did we?"

"I don't think so," Frank replied. "And anyway, there isn't a whole lot we could have told him that he doesn't already know. I wonder how he knew about Bruce rigging that firework? And that question about a cash drain really threw me. Could he possibly know about the extortion?"

Joe shook his head. "Somebody must be telling him things," he said. "But who? The only people who knew about last night were you, me, Matt, and Bruce."

"Plus Grant, plus whoever Matt or Bruce told," Frank pointed out. "What's just as interesting is *why* someone is keeping Morgan informed. The only reason I can think of is to damage the show, but who has a motive to do that?"

Joe fished his key out of his pocket and opened the rear door of the van. "What about Grant's competitors?" he said. "Maybe one of them is out to wreck the show."

"Good thought," Frank said as he climbed into the rear of the van. Joe followed him in and pulled the door closed.

"How about this?" Frank continued. "This

competitor, whoever he is, hires Fat Dave and the motorcycle gang to make trouble for Grant. And the Skulls connect with somebody on the inside who handles the actual sabotage."

"Yeah, but who?" Joe demanded. "Keith? You saw that tattoo. Who'd have that tattoo except somebody connected to the Flying Skulls?"

"We'll have to look into that," Frank agreed, making a note of it on a pad.

"And what about Bruce?" Joe continued. "We did follow him in the direction of the Skulls' clubhouse yesterday. Maybe he was reporting in."

Frank made a face. "That's pretty flimsy," he said. "We don't even know if that's where he was going. He could have had a dozen reasons for heading out that way. Besides, I can't see him sabotaging his own car. That bit with the lost front wheel looked pretty scary to me."

"But what if he *knew* it was going to come off?" Joe insisted. "After all, these guys are pros. Doing things that look scary to the rest of us is part of their jobs."

"Good point," said Frank, making another note on the pad. "But let's not forget Jessica. We may think she's nice, but that sure looked like her on Fat Dave's bike the other day. And I'm still puzzled that she managed to spot that oil on the ramp."

Joe snapped his fingers. "The TV show! Remember? She's supposedly planning a pilot for a

TV series with a motorcycle theme, but nobody knows where the production money is coming from. What if she came up with the extortion plot as a way of raising it? And instead of her working for the Skulls, they're working for her."

"She's not the only one who might be trying to raise a lot of money, though," Frank pointed out. "What if Keith and Bruce are hoping to get their own show going again? They could see this as a great chance to get a lot of money and weaken a future competitor at the same time."

Joe let out a groan. "Come on, Frank" he said. "The last thing we need is more suspects."

Frank chewed the end of his pen for a few moments, then said, "It gets worse, bro. We have to keep in mind that the sabotage and the extortion don't have to be the work of the same person or group. One person might be causing the accidents, while somebody else could be taking advantage of them to extort money from Grant."

Joe looked at him in dismay. "But if that's true," he said, "we have two cases to solve. And we have to solve the extortion case by tonight. How are we going to do it?"

"By being smarter and tougher than the bad guys," Frank said with a grin. "Not to mention harder-working. One place to start is the note. Our guy may have really slipped up by using that old leaflet. And we shouldn't wait for Grant's list of people who were with the show a year ago. We should get out there and ask questions."

Joe glanced out the window. "Look, there's Jessica and Matt, heading out of the arena," he said. "Why not start with them?"

"Good idea," Frank replied, reaching for the door handle.

They intercepted the two on the sidewalk. "Hey, I'm glad we ran into you," Frank said, improvising. "Grant asked us to put together a little history of the show for the TV people, and we need to get some background. You've both been with Grant awhile, haven't you?"

"A couple of years," Jessica replied. "And Matt's been with him even longer."

"Practically since the beginning," the crew chief said. "I was one of the people who helped Tucker put the show on the map. But now I'm not much use to him."

Jessica took his arm. "That's not true, Matt," she said. "Grant kept you on because he needed you. He gave you an important job, didn't he?"

Matt frowned. "Sure, but it's still a big comedown."

"But we're all glad you stayed with the show," Jessica said to Matt. She met Joe's eye. "Matt sounds disappointed sometimes, but he's as loyal as they come."

"That counts for a lot with you, doesn't it, Jess?" Matt said. "It's one of the things I like about you. Listen, can we get moving? I'm hungry, and I've got a busy afternoon ahead."

"Oh, sure," Jessica said. She gave Frank and

Joe an apologetic glance. "Look for me later, and I'll try to help you with that history."

It took Frank a second to remember what she was talking about. "Sure, thanks," he said. Once she and Matt were out of earshot, he turned to Joe. "I wish we'd had a chance to ask about that TV project. I wanted to learn a little more about Jessica's plans."

Joe nodded. "Yeah. But you know one thing I learned?" he asked with a grin. "That it's lunchtime, and I'm starved."

They returned to the van, and Joe drove it to a nearby diner. As they walked in, Joe noticed Chet Morton, their husky, dark-haired friend, in the booth nearest the door. When Chet saw them, he called out, "Hey, if it isn't Frank and Joe Hardy. How are you guys doing? Solved any exciting mysteries this week?"

From a booth a few feet away, Jessica and Matt turned and stared at Joe and Frank.

10 Runaway Truck

Joe slid into the booth next to Chet and said in a low voice, "I'm afraid you just blew our cover."

Chet stared at him with a look of alarm on his face. Then he looked across the table at Frank, who nodded and said, "No doubt about it."

"You mean you're working undercover?"

"That's it," Joe said. "We're—" He noticed the waitress heading for their booth with menus under her arm. He broke off what he was saying to tell her, "I'll have a cheeseburger with everything, fries, and a soda."

"Same here," Frank said.

The waitress noted the orders and left.

"Look," Chet said. "I'm really sorry, guys.

There was no way I could know you were working undercover."

Joe punched him lightly on the shoulder. "Forget about it."

At that moment, Jessica and Matt walked past on their way out with a take-out meal. Jessica met Joe's eyes and gave him a look he couldn't read. Was it anger at being deceived?

"Joe's right," Frank added. "Don't worry about it. You know the hot rod show that's at the arena this weekend? We're investigating an extortion case for the show's promoter. We've been hanging around since Thursday, asking a lot of questions. By now, people must be starting to wonder if we really are press relations trainees, as we said."

Chet popped a french fry into his mouth and said, "Yeah, well, I feel better, but I'm still sorry I blew your cover. Can I make up for it by helping you with the case?"

"Not just now," Frank replied. "Thanks for the offer, though."

"No problem," Chet said. "Anytime."

By the time the Hardys finished their lunch and got up to leave, Chet was trying to decide between lemon meringue and deep-dish apple pie. On the way out to the van, Joe said, "How much time do you think we have before everybody in the company knows what we're really doing?"

Frank gave him a crooked smile and said, "Anywhere from ten to thirty minutes, probably. But maybe it isn't such a disaster. Sure, some people will be more careful about what they say to us. At the same time, our bad guy may decide to back off, knowing that we're watching for him."

As they climbed into the van, Frank added, "Maybe we should take a detour by the Skulls' headquarters on the way back. I'm not sure we've been giving them the attention they deserve."

"Good idea," Joe replied. He took a right out of the diner parking lot and headed toward Buchanan Street. A few minutes later, he pulled over to the curb in back of the line of motorcycles parked in front of the Skulls' clubhouse and turned off the ignition.

Joe saw that the biker with the goatee and ponytail was once again sitting on the front porch. When he spotted the van, he stood up and called over his shoulder. His chair fell backward onto the floor. A moment later, half a dozen Skulls came out the front door and stood in a line on the porch, staring in the Hardys' direction.

"Here goes nothing," Joe muttered under his breath as he opened his door and stepped out of the van. He and Frank slowly walked up the sidewalk.

"Well, well," the man with the goatee said, as Joe and Frank started up the steps. "If it isn't our little messenger boys." He gave them a nasty grin. The line of bikers in back of him cracked up.

"We'd like a word with Fat Dave," Joe said. "Is he around?"

"Maybe, maybe not. What do you want?"

"To talk to your leader," Frank said firmly.

"Fat Dave's a busy man," the biker said. "He doesn't have time to shoot the breeze with every fool who comes around."

"Ronny," a voice bellowed from inside. "Bring those guys here."

For a moment, the biker looked rebellious. Then he motioned Joe and Frank up onto the porch. "You heard the man," he said. "This way."

Joe hesitated for a moment in the doorway of the main room and looked around. The hangout was furnished with three old sofas that looked as if they had been found in a trash heap. A huge poster on the wall showed a biker riding a powerful hog over a mountain road, while a bald eagle flew overhead. Tattered motorcycle magazines were scattered across the floor.

From behind, somebody shoved Joe into the room. A moment later, Fat Dave appeared in another doorway.

"You two saved me some trouble," he said. "I was about to come looking for you, and here you are. You got any more free passes for tonight?"

94

"Sorry, I'm afraid not," Frank said. "How'd you like the show last night?"

The gang leader scratched his bulging stomach. "Not bad," he said. "One part was pretty exciting. Of course, it wasn't on the program."

"Yeah," said Joe. "We wanted to talk to you about that. The people in the show are starting to get very nervous, wondering what'll happen next."

"I don't blame them," Fat Dave said. "You start having a run of bad luck, who knows where it might end? Maybe what Tucker needs is better security," Fat Dave added. "Someone who really knows how to deal with trouble."

Joe looked at him sharply. What was that supposed to mean? Had Fat Dave penetrated their cover, too?

"That's not easy," Frank said. "A big show like Grant's involves a lot of people and a lot of equipment. You can't watch everyone all the time."

Fat Dave grinned. From one side of his mouth, a gold tooth glittered. "It's tough," he said. "You know, I was thinking last night. One of Tucker's weak points is crowd control. You got all those citizens crammed into the arena. If something starts happening, like a fight, and people start to freak, it could get very hairy. Tucker ought to think about that and take steps."

"What kind of steps?" Joe asked. "Hire more guards?"

The gang leader pretended to think for a moment. "That's one way," he finally said. "The trouble is, a lot of hot rod and motorcycle fans are what you might call allergic to guys in uniform. If they're told to sit down, they stand up. But let's say you've got guys handling the crowd that the people know about, guys with a reputation, guys they know aren't going to take any guff from anyone. I'd say you'd be cutting your chances of trouble way down."

Frank nodded slowly. "I'll pass your idea on to Grant," he said. "I can see a couple of problems, though. Tonight's the big night. How do we find enough guys like that on six hours' notice? And even if we do, what is it going to cost? The show runs on a pretty tight budget."

Fat Dave spread his hands in front of him. "I can promise to round up fifty guys—I figure that's a minimum—by seven-thirty tonight, and they won't cost Tucker much more than hiring a bunch of guards with nightsticks from an agency. Of course, if everything goes well and he felt like throwing in a bonus . . ."

"I'll pass on what you said when I get back to the arena," Frank said. "But what about the accidents, like Bruce's wheel last night? We'd all feel a lot better if we knew there wouldn't be any more of them."

"I can't help you there," Fat Dave said, still grinning. "It sounds like what you need is a good detective."

Joe felt the blood rise to his cheeks. This time he was positive that the dig was deliberate. But how had Fat Dave learned that he and Frank were investigating?

"That's an idea," Frank said in a level voice. "We'd better get back and let Grant know what you had to say."

"I'll be here for the next hour," Fat Dave replied. "After that, all deals are off."

In the hallway, Frank turned back and said, "By the way, you owe Tucker for the windows of his tow truck. Do you want him to send you a bill?"

For a long moment, Fat Dave stared at him with narrowed eyes. Then his grin returned. "Tell him not to worry," he said. "We'll settle all that in person, one-on-one."

Once inside the van, Joe let his breath out loudly. "You had me wondering there," he said. "I didn't know if we were going to get out of that house in one piece."

"Sorry I couldn't warn you," Frank replied. "But it's important to let these guys know we'll stand up to them. Besides, I needed to get a good look at the back of the hallway."

"Why?" Joe asked as he started up the engine.

"When we went into the house, I noticed a silver crash helmet sitting on a table in the back room. I wanted to see if it was still there. It wasn't."

"Silver? Hmm. Jessica may have shown up before us and left before we could get a look at her. She could have tipped off Fat Dave that we're detectives."

"It looks that way," said Frank. "Which firms up our hunch that she's connected with the Skulls." Picking up the mobile phone, Frank said, "I want to see if Dad is home."

A few minutes later Frank hung up the phone. "Dad got a call this morning from a friend who had heard he wanted information about the Flying Skulls," he reported. "According to him, the owners of the clubhouse have been trying to evict the gang for months, and it looks as if they might succeed. But a couple of weeks ago, Fat Dave approached the owners and asked them to name a price for the place."

Joe whistled. "So it sounds like the gang needs a lot of money quickly," he said. "And I don't think they'd qualify for a bank loan. That's a really good motive for extortion."

"Yes," Frank replied. "But listen—what do you think about this idea of hiring fifty members of the Skulls to help with crowd control tonight? Okay, the way Fat Dave put it, it was the next thing to demanding protection money from us so the Skulls wouldn't pull any tricks tonight. But why? At most, that'll bring in a few thousand dollars. If Fat Dave is expecting to extort a quarter of a million from Grant, why would he bother with small change?"

"As a backup, in case the extortion plot fails," Joe suggested. "And to have his guys on the inside."

Frank nodded. "Maybe. But there's something there that doesn't hang together. It's almost as if Fat Dave was offering to help the show. There must be something in it for him. Something we're missing."

As they were waiting at a red light a few blocks later, Joe noticed a motorcyclist in a silver crash helmet come out of a side street and head in the direction of the arena. "I think Jessica's going to get back before we do," he said, pointing out the vanishing bike to Frank.

A few minutes later, after parking the van and walking into the arena, he discovered that his prediction was right. Jessica, on her motorcycle, was near the stage entrance, talking to Grant. When she saw Joe and Frank coming, she gave them a troubled look. She started her engine but didn't ride off.

"Jessica doesn't like being spied on," Grant announced. "I told her I brought you in to find out who was causing the accidents." He looked from Frank to Joe and raised an eyebrow in warning. The Hardys understood that Grant hadn't mentioned the extortion attempt to Jessica and they didn't intend to mention it themselves.

"I'm sorry we couldn't tell you the real reason we were here," Joe said to Jessica. "But people might not—"

From behind him, Joe heard the roar of a powerful engine. It was becoming louder. He glanced over his shoulder and froze in horror.

A bright blue 4x4 was coming straight toward them. Joe gaped in amazement when he saw that there was no driver at the wheel. In another moment, they would all be crushed!

11 A Daredevil Ride

"Look out!" Joe cried. Spreading his arms wide, he lunged at Frank and Grant, pushing them away from the path of the oncoming truck. Grant stumbled and fell to his knees. Joe saw Frank grab Grant's collar and pull him out of the way. Then the corner of the 4x4's front bumper grazed Frank's thighs, knocking him aside.

Jessica must have seen the danger she was in. She rammed her motorcycle into first gear and twisted the accelerator. Just as she began to move, Joe jumped onto the back of the bike and grabbed her around the waist.

"The truck," he shouted into her ear. "Get me alongside it."

Jessica nodded and swerved toward the 4x4, which was beginning to pick up speed. At the far end of the arena, directly in its path, Joe saw several TV technicians staring in disbelief.

As the bike moved up alongside the pickup, Joe shifted his left hand to Jessica's shoulder and stood up on the footrests. He leaned over and reached for the roll bar, which was located just behind the cab of the 4x4. Joe strained to grab the bar, but the gap was too wide. Jessica realized the problem and inched the bike closer to the side of the truck.

As his fingers touched the smooth chrome of the roll bar, Joe risked a quick glance forward. The motorcycle and truck were already halfway down the length of the arena. In another few moments, the 4x4 would crash into the concrete barrier that surrounded the track.

Desperately he clenched his right hand around the roll bar and took a mad leap off the back of the motorcycle. He gasped in alarm as his hand began to slip. He looked down and saw the big rear wheel of the 4x4 looming only inches behind him. If he fell, he could never manage to avoid it. The tire would flatten him into the dust.

Suddenly he remembered a circus act he had once seen, a bareback rider who leapt down from his horse and somehow jumped back up. Would it work for him? He had to try. It was his only chance.

Joe let his feet touch the floor and used the momentum it gave him to push his body upward. Twisting at the waist, he managed to fling his right leg over the side wall of the pickup's bed. He lunged forward, climbed through the open window of the cab, and grabbed for the shift lever and hand brake. The tires screeched, and the powerful engine roared in protest as he yanked it out of gear. Then he found the ignition key and turned it off.

Silence. Joe took a deep breath and pushed himself into a sitting position. Through the windshield, he saw a platform loaded with TV equipment only ten feet from the front of the truck. The technicians had scattered.

Jessica's motorcycle roared up and skidded to a stop. "Joe!" she called. "Are you all right?"

He answered with a thumbs-up sign and a weak grin.

Frank and Grant came running up. "Wow!" the promoter exclaimed. "That was terrific. Listen, Joe, any time you want a job with the show, it's yours. I just wish the TV guys had caught some footage."

Joe caught Frank's eye and shook his head in amazement. Grant seemed to see everything that happened as just another stunt. Was it possible that he was causing the accidents himself, for the sake of publicity? Joe wondered. Probably not, he decided. The promoter had been standing in front of the 4x4 himself. If Joe had been even a tiny bit less alert, Grant could have been seriously hurt. Would anyone take that kind of risk just to get a mention on the evening news?

Grant pulled the door open and climbed up into the cab next to Joe. Bending down, he peered at the dashboard and said, "I thought so. This was no accident. Somebody aimed the truck at us and set the hand throttle, then bailed out. We're lucky someone didn't get killed."

"That wasn't luck," Jessica said. She pulled her helmet off and shook out her blond hair. "Joe's quick moves saved the day." Smiling at him, she said, "Did you ever consider a career in a hot rod show?"

Feeling a bit embarrassed, Joe said, "Hey, it was nothing." He was happy to see that Jessica seemed to have forgotten he was a snoop and decided he was a hero instead.

From the stage entrance, eight or ten members of the company came running. Joe noticed both Keith and Bruce among them, along with Matt, who seemed to be limping more than usual.

A short-haired guy wearing a Keep On Truckin' T-shirt was in the lead. "Hey," he called as he came up to them, "what's going on here? Who's been messing with my rig?"

"That's what we'd like to know, Walt," said

Grant. "It nearly killed us. Where did you leave it?"

The guy looked away from Grant at the semi-circle that was forming. "In the staging area, near the entrance," he said, shifting from one foot to the other. "The motor felt a little ragged, so I asked Matt to check the timing for me. Right, Matt?" he called.

The crew chief hurried up to the group. "That's right," he said. He wiped his palms on the legs of his oil-stained white coveralls. "I listened to it for myself, then went off to get the timing light. When I came back, the truck wasn't there. I figured Walt must have changed his mind and driven it back to the garage. Then I heard all the commotion."

"Was there anyone else nearby when you left to get the timing light?" Frank asked.

Matt frowned. "I'm not answering any questions from you," he said. "You or your brother. I don't talk to spies."

Grant faced him. "Oh, yes, you do, if you want to keep your job," he said. "And that goes for the rest of you, too."

For a moment, Joe thought that Matt was going to turn and walk off. Then some of his defiance seemed to leave him. "Oh, okay," he said. "I didn't take any particular notice, but I remember seeing Keith going in the direction of the truck as I walked away."

"Now, hold on there," Keith said loudly, pushing forward. "If you're trying to say I'm responsible for this, you're a liar. I never touched this truck."

Joe jumped in. "But you did pass near it?"

"Well . . . I guess so," Keith replied. "I was going to the parking lot from the dressing rooms, so I had to go through the staging area. But I don't remember noticing either Matt or Walt's four-by."

Joe pressed him. "Do you remember anything at all that caught your attention? Anything that seemed odd or out of place?"

Keith looked troubled. "Not at that point, no. But a couple of minutes later, I happened to look around and, well, I thought I saw somebody all in black disappearing around the corner in the direction of the dressing rooms."

Everyone looked around. Only one person was wearing all black—Bruce Sears.

For a moment, Bruce didn't seem to realize why everyone was staring at him. Then his face reddened and he clenched his fists. "Why, you slimy . . ." he said, taking a step in Keith's direction. "Are you trying to say that *I* rigged Walt's truck to run over these people?"

"I didn't say that," Keith said unhappily. "I didn't see the guy's face, just his back. And I don't even know if he had anything to do with this. I saw him walking away, that's all. That was when I heard the shouts. And I remember wondering why he didn't turn around to find out what was going on."

"Maybe he already knew," Frank suggested. "Bruce, do you mind telling us where you were when you heard the commotion out here?"

"You bet I mind," Bruce said loudly. "I mind a whole lot. But I'll tell you anyway. I was coming from my dressing room."

Joe asked, "Did you notice anybody else around at that point?"

"What is this, cops and robbers?" Bruce demanded. "Yeah, I saw Matt come out of the toolroom with a timing light in his hand. I remember, because the timing light looks a lot like a pistol, and for a second I thought it really was one."

Joe looked over at Matt, who was fiddling with the zipper of his coveralls. "Matt?" Joe said. "Did you see Bruce?"

Matt scowled and shook his head. "No, I . . . He must have been in back of me. I don't know. I've already told you everything I can."

"Just one more question," Frank said. "Did you have any trouble finding the timing light?"

"The timing light?" the crew chief repeated. "No. It was in the top of one of the tool chests, right next to the door. I just picked it up and came out, and that's when I heard all the yelling."

Grant looked at Joe and Frank. "Anything else?" he asked. They shook their heads. "Okay," Grant said in a louder voice. "That's it. Let's get back to work. Tonight's a big night."

"You mean I can take my rig now?" Walt inquired. "I want to make sure nobody damaged it. And I still want the timing checked."

The group broke up. As Grant started to walk away, Frank stopped him and told him about Fat Dave's offer.

"Crowd control, huh?" Grant said, rubbing his chin. "I get the picture. Either I pay, or else. Still . . . I think I can live with that. I'll go give him a call."

"What do you think?" Joe asked softly, once he and Frank were alone. "Matt? Keith? Bruce? Or a mysterious man in black?"

"Any of the above," Frank replied. "The only people we're sure didn't do it are Grant and Jessica, because they were both with us."

"So that puts Jessica in the clear," said Joe. "And just when she was starting to look like a good suspect."

Frank frowned. "She's in the clear on this latest happening," he said. "She still might be involved in some of the rest of the stuff that's going on. And the same goes for Grant, by the way."

He paused and gazed out across the empty arena. "I think we ought to take a closer look at the dressing rooms and the staging area. I'm having trouble visualizing everybody's movements."

The blue 4x4 was standing near the entrance tunnel with the hood up and the engine running. Joe made a point of not walking in front of it. Someone was bent over the fender doing something to the engine. Frank tapped him on the shoulder and he straightened up. It was Walt.

"Is this about where your truck was before?" asked Frank.

Walt glanced around. "Yeah, yeah," he said. "Pretty much so."

Frank stepped away from the truck and eyed the distance to the corridor that led to the dressing rooms. "I wonder . . ." he said, starting toward the dressing rooms. Joe followed.

"This must be Matt's room," Frank said, stopping outside the first door. He tried the knob. It was unlocked. He pushed the door open and switched on the light.

Joe peered over his shoulder. Five or six rolling tool chests were scattered around. A couple of sets of coveralls lay on a folding metal chair.

"Somebody does really fine work," Frank said, pointing to the workbench in the corner.

Joe looked and saw three carefully detailed models of classic hot rods carved in wood. "Matt?" he suggested.

"Must be," Frank responded. "This is his

room. And this must be the famous timing light," he added, picking it up. "I wonder—"

A faint *peep! peep!* interrupted him. For a moment, neither he nor Joe reacted. Then Frank exclaimed, "The beeper! Come on—somebody's trying to break into the van!"

12 The Man in Black

Frank sprinted across the staging area and ran along the loading dock to the steps. He could hear Joe right behind him. As they neared the parking lot Frank stopped and held out his arm.

"Let's separate," he said quickly. "You go right, I'll go left. We'll try to trap him between us."

"Check." Joe crouched down and ran for the shelter of the right-hand row of parked cars.

Frank watched Joe run, then scurried behind the row of cars on the left.

The van was seven or eight cars in from the access lane. Frank passed four cars, then paused behind a small sedan and peered through its windows. The van's roof loomed up over the tops of its neighbors. He couldn't see anyone near it. Had something scared off the would-be burglar, or was he simply keeping out of sight?

Still crouching down, Frank moved along the length of the sedan and crept toward the van. Suddenly, from behind him, he heard the faint sound of a shoe scraping on the pavement. He started to turn. But in that very instant he felt a terrible shock at the base of his skull and saw the gray asphalt of the parking lot rushing up toward his face.

Something was shaking Frank's shoulder. Each tiny movement sent a new wave of pain through his head. He groaned and tried to push away the attacker who kept shaking him and setting off bombs in his ear.

The explosions became words. "Frank, Frank, Frank!" Then he remembered. *He* was Frank, and the words were coming from his brother, Joe.

He opened his eyes and saw pavement that seemed to stretch to the horizon. A little to the left of the endless expanse were a running shoe and a denim-clad knee.

"Frank," Joe's voice repeated. "Are you all right?"

Frank tried to say, "I'm fine," but all that came out was another groan.

"Don't try to move," Joe said. "I'll call for an ambulance."

Frank took a deep breath and tried again to speak. "No," he managed to say. "I'm okay. One

112

minute." After two more deep breaths, Frank placed his palms on the rough asphalt and pushed. It was like trying to push a solid wall. Dizzy, he forced himself into a sitting position, then shut his eyes tight against the glare of the sky.

Frank felt his brother's arm firm around his shoulders, keeping him from falling over again. "I'm calling a doctor," Joe said.

Frank opened his eyes. "No," he repeated. "I'll be okay." He reached up and carefully touched the bump at the base of his skull. To his fingers, it felt huge, somewhere near the size of a baseball, but he knew from experience that it wasn't that bad.

"Did you see him?" he demanded. "The guy who hit me?"

"I was too far away to get a good look," Joe admitted. "All I can tell you is that he was dressed completely in black and he ran back inside the arena. Oh, and he slashed one of the front tires on the van."

In response to Frank's sound of angry disgust, Joe added, "It could have been worse. If we hadn't shown up when we did, he might have slashed all four."

"Help me up," Frank said grimly. "We've got to get that tire changed fast. He must really want to keep us immobilized, or he wouldn't have taken the risk of slashing our tire in broad daylight."

Getting up, Frank clung to Joe's arm and clenched his teeth against the pain. Once he was standing, he felt a little better. "You change the tire," he joked. "I'll give you the benefit of my expert advice."

While Joe found and brought out the spare tire, jack, lug wrench, and tire iron, Frank leaned against the fender of the next car and tried to remember if he'd seen anyone right before he'd been knocked out.

After Joe tapped the hubcap back into place, he rolled the flat tire around to the rear of the van. As he was lifting it in, he glanced around, then suddenly said in a low, firm voice, "Frank, down."

Frank unlocked his knees and let himself slide down the side of the car he had been leaning on. "What is it?" he asked in a whisper.

"Keith and Bruce just came out of the arena," Joe replied. "They're heading for Keith's car. We've got to find out where they're going. Do you need help getting into the van?"

"I'll manage," Frank said. Bent down, he made his way to the passenger door. Using the handle to pull himself upright, he wrestled the door open. As he slumped into the seat and closed his eyes, he felt the van pull out of its slot and accelerate toward the parking lot exit.

Hardly any time seemed to pass before he heard Joe say, "They're turning in at the fried chicken place. All that trouble, just to watch two guys have their dinner.''

Frank sat up in his seat and opened his eyes. Keith and Bruce had just entered the fast-food restaurant. Through the big plate glass windows, he saw them choose a booth toward the back. "I've got a hunch about this," he said. "Those guys have supposedly been at each other's throats for weeks. I can't believe they're burying the hatchet over a basket of chicken and fries.''

"Hoo, boy!" Joe exclaimed. "Will you take a look at that cruisemobile.''

Frank turned his head. A stretch limousine with darkened windows had just driven into the parking lot. The driver didn't even bother trying to fit the huge vehicle into one of the slots. Instead, he simply pulled up at the curb, not caring that he was blocking five parking places.

The man who stepped out of the rear door wore an off-white suit, a bright turquoise shirt open at the neck, and half a dozen glittering gold chains. A pair of expensive sunglasses hid his eyes. He glanced around the parking lot, then walked over to the restaurant entrance.

"Any bets on where he's going?" Joe murmured.

"No bets," Frank replied. "I just wish we had a bug at their table.''

The newcomer strolled through the restaurant and slid into the booth across from Keith and

Bruce. When the waitress came over, he motioned her away. He talked for a few minutes, waving his arms and nodding, then stood up and shook hands with the two hot-rodders.

"Duck," Frank said, as the man came out and walked over to his limo. "After him! We've got to find out who he is."

"I'll stick to him like glue," Joe promised. He started the engine of the van and slipped the gear lever into drive.

As they followed the limo, Frank had to admire the driver's skill. He was fast but smooth, drifting almost casually from one lane to another and always ending up in the one that was moving best. Clearly a real pro.

As they neared the expressway entrance, Joe said, "I hope he's not driving all the way into the city. We've got to be at the arena for the show tonight."

"We'll split up if we have to," Frank replied. "You can drop me off, and I'll get a cab to the arena. But I don't think I'll need to. He's not turning onto the expressway, after all."

"Then where's he going?" Joe asked. "There's nothing much out this way. Oh, wait, there's that fancy motel that opened last month. He must be staying there."

A few moments later, Frank spotted the big motel sign up ahead. "That's the place," Frank said.

Joe slowed down. Frank watched the stretch

116

limo turn into the motel driveway. The car glided past the swimming pool and came to a stop next to a small building separated from the rest of the complex by hedges.

Joe pulled around to the visitors' parking area, just in front of the office. "How do we play this?" he asked Frank.

Frank rubbed his head, then winced as he touched the bump on the back. "Um—how about reporters for the college paper?" he suggested.

"Sounds good to me," Joe replied. He fished a steno pad and ballpoint pen from the glove compartment. "Let's go."

Inside, a young woman in a black skirt and white blouse was standing behind the counter. She looked up from sorting a stack of receipts and smiled. "Good afternoon," she said. "Can I help you?"

Frank returned the smile and explained that he and Joe were trying out for a position with the college newspaper.

"We're thinking of doing a story about some of the important new businesses in Bayport," he said. "And this seemed like a good place to start."

"Oh, it certainly is," the young woman replied warmly. "This is the first really up-to-date facility for today's business traveler in the whole area. Here, let me get you a copy of the brochure."

A moment later, she was showing Frank and

117

Joe color photos of the conference rooms and explaining the audiovisual and teleconferencing options that were offered.

"This is great," Frank finally said, tucking the brochure in his back pocket. "I bet, with a setup like this, that you're already starting to draw important guests."

"Oh, absolutely," the young woman said. "Of course, our guests expect us to respect their privacy, but just between us, we've had top people from some of the biggest corporations in the country staying here. And you know what? Most of them are just as nice as you could ask."

Joe turned away from the window and said, "When we drove in, the biggest limo I've ever seen turned in just ahead of us. I told Frank it had to be some TV star, but he thought it was probably a banker or something."

"I'm afraid you're both wrong," the young woman replied. "That's Bart Preston, the big promoter. He's in the Imperial Suite, which has its own sauna, whirlpool, and tanning room."

"Bart Preston," Frank repeated. "I've heard that name somewhere."

"Of course you have. There's a stack of leaflets for his new auto show on the table by the door. You should pick one up."

Joe glanced at his watch. "Uh-oh. We have to run. Thanks for your help."

"You're very welcome," she replied. "And if

it's not too much trouble, send me a copy of your story when it comes out."

In the van, Frank and Joe studied the leaflet. It advertised The World's Greatest Hot Rod and Custom Show, which was coming the following month to a nearby town. At the bottom, in bold type, it promised a surprise appearance by the two greatest drag-racing rivals in the world. Frank and Joe stared at each other, growing excited.

"So that's it," Joe said. "Bruce and Keith are planning to leave Grant and take their act over to Preston's show. They were meeting Preston today to work out the details."

"It sure looks that way," said Frank. "Which means that they've been working together the whole time. All their arguments and fights were just an act, to build up the idea of their rivalry."

Joe made a disgusted noise. "Now I see why most of the so-called accidents were aimed at them," he said. "Because they were setting them up themselves. Wait'll we tell Grant that this whole case is nothing more than a giant publicity stunt—for another promoter."

13 Trapped!

"What now?" Joe asked, as he drove toward the arena. "Do we go find Keith and Bruce and make them confess?"

"The only evidence we have is Preston's leaflet and their meeting with him," Frank said. "They'd probably laugh at us. Anyway, there are still a lot of questions we don't know the answers to. Let's say that Keith and Bruce planned to stage a series of what appear to be accidents in order to get publicity. Does that mean they've been behind all the sabotage? What about the oil on the ramp? How would it have helped them if Jessica had been hurt?"

Joe nodded. "I see your point," he said. "And we've still got our main mystery to solve, too.

Who's trying to extort a quarter of a million bucks from Grant? We figured the sabotage was part of the extortion plot. Does that mean that Bruce and Keith are the extortionists? Or is somebody else using the sabotage to extort money?"

"There's another possibility," said Frank. "Maybe Bruce and Keith's accidents inspired the extortionist to stage a few of his own. Don't forget the mysterious man in black. If Keith and Bruce are really partners, it doesn't make sense for Keith to accuse Bruce of sending that four-by-four at us. So it seems likely that Keith really did see someone in black, and that he's the one who tried to run us over."

"And who tried to knock your head off in the parking lot," Joe added.

"Ouch, don't remind me!" Frank exclaimed, touching the back of his head. "You know, I just had a very weird idea. Nothing in this case is turning out to be what it seems. Well, what about that 4x4? The guy must have aimed it at us, set the hand throttle, and bailed out. Why didn't he set it for a higher speed, then? He could have, just as easily, and we would have had a lot more trouble getting out of the way."

"Are you saying that it was another hoax, like the stuff that's happened to Keith and Bruce?"

"No, just that it may not have been as serious an attack as it looked," Frank replied. "Maybe you and I and Grant were *meant* to get away. Or Grant, at least. After all, without Grant around,

121

the extortionist can't hope to get his money. But here's an even weirder idea. What if the whole extortion plot is a fake?"

"Come on," Joe said. "Grant showed us the note. You're not saying that he's extorting money from himself."

"Why not? Remember what Dad told us about the accusations against him. What better way to divert a lot of money from the show into his own pocket than to turn it over to a mythical extortion-ist?"

Joe folded his arms and studied his brother for a moment, then said, "Maybe that bang over the head was more serious than I thought. Are you sure you're playing with a full deck?"

"I told you it was a weird idea," Frank said with a laugh. "But it's worth keeping in mind. And let's not forget our motorcycle friends. They may or may not be trying to extort money from Grant, but I guarantee you, they're no angels."

Although it was still a couple of hours before the doors opened for the evening show, the parking lot of the Bayport Arena was already starting to fill up. Joe found an empty slot in the staff section and pulled in.

"This is too complicated," he announced, reaching for the door handle. "Let's go look for Bruce and Keith. At least we can take a shot at clearing up one part of this case."

The guard at the staff entrance recognized the Hardys from all of their coming and going. As he waved them past his desk, the guard said, "This place is going nuts. Would you believe a whole gang of bikers just walked in? They said they were here to handle crowd control. If I ever saw a crowd that needed controlling, they're it."

As Frank and his brother walked down the corridor toward the staging area, Joe murmured, "It sounds like Grant and Fat Dave made a deal. I hope nobody's sorry later on."

Joe found the staging area jammed with cars, motorcycles, and people. A TV crew was edging through the crowd, stopping to interview drivers and mechanics or to take close-ups of the gleaming machines. Every minute or so, an engine roared to life, then shut down.

Joe scanned the big room, looking for either Keith or Bruce. He spotted Jessica, in her silver jumpsuit, across the room. She was talking to Matt, who was pulling on a white coverall. Her shoulders looked very tense. Was she worried about doing her act for live TV? Joe wondered.

"No sign of Keith or Bruce," Frank murmured. "I don't see their cars, either. Let's check the arena. Maybe they're practicing."

Joe followed his brother through the entrance tunnel and out onto the concrete. Keith's slingshot dragster was nearby. He was already in the driver's seat, talking to an admiring group of Flying Skulls. As the Hardys drew closer, he fired up the engine, which idled with a sound like an approaching thunderstorm.

Frank stepped up to Keith, leaned close, and said, "We have to talk to you."

"Later," Keith shouted.

Frank shook his head vigorously. "Now," he said. He pulled the Bart Preston leaflet from his pocket and held it in Keith's line of sight.

Keith's eyes widened as he realized what Frank and Joe had figured out. His hands gripped the wheel tighter, and his foot pressed the accelerator. The huge supercharged V-8 let out an anguished roar. Frank, Joe, and the other spectators jumped for safety as the dragster began to scream down the track. Then, even above the sound of the engine, they heard a *whoosh!* An instant later, the dragster was hidden by a sheet of flame.

Without stopping to think, Joe sprinted toward the burning dragster. As he drew closer, he shielded his face with his bent arm. He thought he saw Keith stand up in the driver's cockpit and jump out. Then he lost sight of him. Bent almost double, Joe continued toward the flames and spotted a crumpled form on the pavement. He blindly grabbed something, which turned out to be a boot, and dragged Keith away from the searing heat.

Then Frank ran over to Joe and pulled him to safety. Someone dumped a bucket of cool water over Joe's head. He shook the water off his face and looked back. A circle of bikers and crew members was spraying foam on the dragster. The flames were already out.

"Keith?" Joe said, panting. "Is he okay?"

"I'm fine, thanks to you and my flameproof long johns," Keith said.

"Was this another of your stunts?" Joe demanded. "Because if it was, I'm going to knock you halfway into next week."

"I've put years of work into that car," Keith replied. "I'd never risk it like that. No, somebody else did this, and I'd like to know who."

"Could it have been a real accident?" Frank asked.

"Not a chance," Keith said. "My hunch is that there was some kind of container of fuel—gas or methanol—wedged against the engine. The engine got hot, the container shattered, and I almost roasted."

Bruce came running over. "I just heard," he gasped. "Are you—?"

"I'm fine," Keith said. "I was just telling Joe and Frank that I think our little jokes inspired somebody to play for keeps."

"Why did you say that?" Bruce shouted.

"It's okay. They figured it out for themselves," Keith said wearily. "They know about Preston, too." He looked up at Frank. "Have you told Grant yet?"

The promoter came up just in time to hear. "Told Grant what?" he demanded. "Matt just said your car'll be okay with a little work, if that's what you mean."

"That's not it," Keith replied. "The feud between me and Bruce was all a gag to boost our ratings. We staged some of the accidents, too, and tipped off Bob Morgan about them. And we've been talking with Preston about signing up with his outfit."

Joe expected Grant to explode with anger. Instead, he said, "Oh? It sounds like you two are going after the world record for bonehead moves. Do you really think you'll be better off in Preston's show? Oh, never mind. We'll talk about that later." Turning to the Hardys, he said, "Frank, Joe, I need you."

As they walked away, Joe noticed Bob Morgan heading toward Keith and Bruce. He was about to get quite a story.

Grant put one arm around Frank's shoulders and the other around Joe's, pulling their heads close to his. "I just got a call," he said softly. "I have to deliver the money at ten o'clock tonight. The guy said that what happened to Keith was just a warning. I didn't even know what he meant until I came down to find you."

"Ten o'clock," Frank repeated. "Right before several thousand spectators all try to leave the arena at once. Did your caller say where?"

"Yeah," Grant said, nodding. "It's to be left on the front seat of Mike Carrigan's hot rod, in the storage area. That's a maroon '51 Mercury coupe, chopped and channeled, with flame treatment on the sides and a Jimmy blower on the mill."

All the jargon threw Joe. "No kidding?" he said. "What does that mean?"

"Sorry," Grant replied. "The body and the roof have been lowered, and there's a big supercharger sticking up through the hood."

"Oh. Okay. What about this Carrigan guy?"

Grant shook his head. "Nothing to do with him. He's been out of the show for a couple of weeks, doing some stunt driving for a movie company out west."

Frank frowned. "You said, '*I* have to deliver the money.' Did the caller tell you to do it personally?"

Grant hesitated. "I don't think so," he finally said. "No, as long as it's all there, I don't think he cares who delivers it."

"All right, then," Frank continued. "When ten o'clock rolls around, I'll make the drop myself. And Joe will already be in position, watching to see who picks it up."

"And I," Grant said grimly, "will be waiting for my chance to tear that creep, whoever he is, into tiny pieces. *After* I get my money back."

Joe shifted his weight onto his left side and tried to massage the cramp out of his right shoulder. His father had once said that the worst part of detective work was stakeouts. Joe was beginning to agree.

The hiding place he had chosen was the bed of

a 4x4 pickup. Its position, not far from the maroon Mercury, was perfect, and he didn't have to worry about courtesy lights coming on when he opened the door. But who would have thought a pickup bed would have so many hard edges to dig into your ribs and knees, Joe thought, and so many angles to bump your head against?

He pushed up his sleeve and peered at his watch. Nine fifty-eight. Frank should be coming with the money any time now. Joe wondered who the extortionist would turn out to be. Not Bruce or Keith, he was pretty sure of that. And he didn't think much of Frank's crazy idea that Grant was using the plot to divert money from the show. Fat Dave, or one of his guys? Possibly, but Joe was ready to bet on the man in black. And he was starting to have a hunch who he was.

A door slammed at the far end of the storage area. Joe ducked lower behind the tailgate as footsteps approached. The ceiling light came on in the old Mercury. He saw Frank place a large brown bag on the front seat, look around, and slam the door. Then his footsteps retreated rapidly.

From the arena came a faint sound of cheers and applause. As it died away, Joe heard a tiny scraping sound from off to his left. He peered into the shadowy gap between two cars and saw something moving, something that glittered in the dim light. It moved toward the hot rod with the money in the front seat. Joe felt sick. He could not mistake that silver jumpsuit or that head of blond hair.

There was no point in hiding any longer. He had found out what he needed to know. As Jessica reached for the hot rod's door handle, Joe got to his feet, vaulted over the sidewall of the pickup, and walked toward her. At the sound, she whirled around in alarm.

"It's me," he said. "Joe Hardy."

"Joe!" Jessica exclaimed. "What are you doing here?"

Behind him, something moved. Joe looked down and glimpsed a black pant leg. He started to turn and caught a glimpse of something coming toward his head, fast. There was just enough time to lurch forward and hunch his shoulders. Then a fireworks display exploded inside his skull.

When Joe woke up, it was dark and stuffy, and he was lying curled up with what felt like a bag of sand half on top of him. Something hard was jutting into his back, just between the shoulder blades. He tried to stretch out his legs and uncurl his neck, but there was something unyielding in both directions.

He felt around. The bag of sand was warm and breathing. He touched the head and thought he recognized Jessica's hair. She must not be the extortionist, Joe assumed. But what had she been doing in the storage area? And why was she here with him now, wherever they might be? He shook her shoulder, but there was no response at all.

He tried to sit up and cried out in pain as his head slammed into something hard, only a few inches above him. For a moment panic threatened to take over. Horror stories about being buried alive flitted through his mind.

"This is obviously the trunk of a car," Joe said to himself, feeling around in the dark. But whose car was it, and how would he and Jessica get out?

14 Under Bigfoot

When Frank returned to the work area, he found
Grant waiting for him near the tunnel that led out
into the arena. The promoter had one eye on the
arena and the other on the work area, where the
next acts to go on were getting ready. He glanced
at Frank and asked, "Any hitches?"

"Not so far," Frank replied. "Did you tell the
guard not to let anybody leave by the performers'
entrance?"

"Yeah. I even locked the door to the parking
lot. I hope the fire inspector doesn't find out." He
looked out at the arena. "It's been a super show
so far. The TV audiences will eat it up. Watch
your back."

Frank flattened himself against the wall to let

131

two big 4x4 trucks come offstage after the hill climb event. A minute or two later, a team of acrobatic clowns riding a motorcycle and sidecar zipped by in the other direction. They were greeted with cheers.

Frank watched them for a few minutes, but he was starting to get nervous. Where was Joe? They had agreed that he would come find Frank and Grant the moment he had identified the extortionist. But what was taking so long? Had something gone wrong with their plan?

As the clowns were coming offstage, one of the tech crew hurried up to Grant. "Jessica hasn't shown up yet," he said. "And she's on next, after the lowriders."

"Did you check her dressing room?" Grant asked.

"She's not there," the man replied. "And her engine's cold. You know how she is about warming up before her act."

Frank straightened up. "I don't like this. There's been some kind of foul-up," he told Grant. "I'm going to go see what's happened to my brother."

"And my money," Grant added.

The storage room was dark and silent. Frank found the light switch and flipped it on. He hurried down the row of cars to the maroon hot rod and bent over to peer into the front seat.

As he expected, the money bag was gone.

He was about to straighten up when he noticed

something else. Tucked into the crack of the front seat, barely in sight, was a wide wristband. He fished it out and examined it. Pointed silver studs lined the borders, and in the center, carved into the black leather, was a skull with wings.

"Fat Dave," Frank muttered to himself. He set out at a run for the arena entrance.

Grant stepped in front of him, barring the way. "Well?" he said anxiously.

"We've got a problem," Frank said. "The money's gone, and I can't find Joe. This was on the front seat of the car."

Grant glanced at the wristband. His face reddened, and his neck seemed to swell up. "Come with me," he said, and charged out into the arena.

A line of lowriders was circling the performance space, while two others, in the center, were using their hydraulic suspension systems to bounce high into the air. Grant led Frank around the perimeter to the judges' stand. Fat Dave was standing next to the platform, his thumbs tucked into his wide studded belt.

"I need to talk to you," Grant said to the gang leader. "I thought we had a deal."

"So did I," Fat Dave replied. "You have some kind of problem?"

"Some creep just took me for a quarter of a million bucks. He left this behind." Grant showed him the wristband.

Fat Dave looked at it with narrowed eyes.

"That fool is asking for lots of grief," he said. "The Skulls don't like frame-ups."

"Are you saying this isn't yours?" Frank asked.

The bearded biker shrugged. "Oh, sure, it's Billy's," he replied. "He lost it the other day, when we did our little parade outside here. He wasn't too happy about it, either. He'd had it made up special."

"The extortionist must have found it," Frank said to Grant. "He left it in the car tonight, hoping to throw us off his trail."

Fat Dave gave him a puzzled look.

"We've got to find Joe," Frank continued, not wanting to explain about the extortionist just yet. "I'm sure he's in danger. Fat Dave, will your guys help us search backstage?"

"If it'll lead us to the loser who tried to frame us, sure." He put two fingers to his lips and gave a piercing whistle, then circled his fist in the air. From all over the arena, members of the Flying Skulls started making their way toward the judges' platform.

Frank led his new band of helpers toward the work area. As they passed through the entrance tunnel, the same techie who had spoken to Grant earlier hurried over. "Still no sign of Jessica," he reported.

"Scratch her act," the promoter said. "We'll go straight from the lowriders to Bigfoot."

"Check," the man replied. "I'll alert the tow

truck to get the junkers into position as soon as the lowriders come off."

Frank tugged at Grant's sleeve. "Has Jessica ever missed her act before?"

"Never. She's a real trouper."

"It can't be a coincidence that she's turned up missing at the same time the extortion money has disappeared," Frank said.

Grant stared at him. "Jessica? Not a chance. I'd suspect myself before I'd suspect her."

"Well, whoever our extortionist might be, we'd better post somebody here, at the entrance to the arena, in case he or she tries to mingle with the audience and escape that way."

"Right," said Grant, and spoke to the techie.

"What do you want us to do?" Fat Dave demanded.

"We'd better search the whole backstage area, starting with the dressing rooms," Frank replied. "We're looking for my brother, Joe, and for Jessica Derey—you know who she is, don't you?"

"Yeah, we know," Fat Dave said.

"Okay," Frank continued. "And we're also looking for a paper bag full of used tens and twenties."

"Any reward for finding it?" the Skulls' leader asked.

Grant said, "Don't sweat it. Anybody who finds my money won't be sorry he did."

"Okay, you heard the man," Fat Dave called to his gang. "Fan out and get to work."

While the Skulls went off to search the dressing rooms, Frank double-checked with the guard at the staff entrance. The guard said he was sure that no one had gone out to the parking lot, and he promised not to let anyone do so. The door was still locked, just as Grant had left it.

"We've got him cornered now," Frank said. "All we need to do is find Joe and Jessica—"

"And the money," Grant interjected.

"And identify the extortionist," Frank continued. "It sounds simple enough. I just wish I didn't feel so uneasy. Come on, let's join the search."

As they approached the work area, Bob Morgan came running over and grabbed Grant's arm. "What's going on?" he demanded. "I heard somebody's missing, along with a lot of money."

"Stick around and keep your ears open," Grant told the reporter, brushing past him.

Bruce and Keith were standing near the front of Bruce's Deuce roadster. They looked as if they had been arguing.

"Hey, Grant," Bruce called. "Will you settle something for us?"

"Later," Grant replied.

"It'll just take a sec," Bruce insisted. "I told Keith that, since he doesn't have wheels just now, he should ride with me in the final parade."

"And I said I want a car of my own," Keith said.

Grant rolled his eyes. "Look, you guys are supposed to be feuding, right?" he said. "So don't go out there looking like best buddies. Keith, you can drive my GTO in the parade. I'll tell Matt to get it ready."

He looked around. "Hey, anybody seen Matt?" he shouted.

The crew chief appeared in the doorway of the toolroom. He had a toolbox in one hand, and with the other, he was zipping up his coveralls.

"Here I am," he called. "What do you need?"

While Grant started to explain about the GTO, Frank looked around the busy, noisy work area. The tow truck was pulling another junker out of the storage area, ready to take it into the arena for Bigfoot's act. From the direction of the dressing rooms, a little group of Skulls appeared, looking discouraged.

"Sure, I'll take care of it right now," Matt told Grant.

"Good." Grant reached for the toolbox in Matt's hand. "I'll put this back for you," he said.

"No." Matt pulled away. "It's okay, I'm going to need it in a minute." He limped off toward the garage.

"Too bad about him," Grant remarked. "He's a good mechanic, no question. But he was a great stunt rider. He still could be, if that crash hadn't made him lose his nerve and turn sour."

"What about his knee?" asked Frank. "Was there some reason it couldn't be fixed?"

Grant shook his head. "That's just an excuse. I told him the company would pay for the operation. The truth is, he feels better, staying safe in the background and resenting everybody who's out in the spotlight. I think he's afraid to ride again. Oh, well, come on. We've got work to do."

Fat Dave joined them. "Nothing in the dressing rooms or the toolroom," he reported. "What next? The garage?"

Frank nodded and started for the big sliding doors, with Grant, Fat Dave, and the Skulls behind him. They stepped aside to let the tow truck bring out the last of the junkers, then entered the echoing storage room and began to search.

It didn't take very long. Most of the show's stable of hot rods and 4x4 trucks were being used in the performance. Finally Frank slammed the lid of the last empty trunk and said, "That's it. There's no sign of them anywhere."

"But that's impossible," Grant said. "We know they didn't leave the backstage area. We've got people watching the exits. Nothing's gone in or out."

Frank looked around. One of the lowriders caught his eye. "Wait," he said. "That's not true. That car went out, into the arena, and came back. So did the other lowriders."

"Yeah," said Fat Dave. "But we just searched them. They're clean."

"What about the cars that are in the arena now?" Frank asked. "We didn't search them."

"There aren't any," Grant replied. "The only vehicle out there now is Bigfoot."

Staring at him in growing horror, Frank said, "Bigfoot . . . and the cars that Bigfoot is about to crush."

15 The Man in
Black Revealed

Frank ran at top speed across the storage area and into the tunnel that led to the arena. If his hunch was right, Joe was trapped in one of the cars that Bigfoot would soon turn to scrap metal. Behind him he heard Grant and the Skulls following him. As Frank neared the arena, someone stepped in front of him.

"Hold on, you can't go—"

Frank dodged past the outstretched arm and kept running into the arena. The brilliant floodlights dazzled him. He paused, narrowed his eyes against the glare, and looked around frantically.

Bigfoot was at the far end of the arena, beginning to turn for a run down the center of the track. In the center of the arena, parked side by

140

side, were the dozen sedans that the monster 4x4 was about to drive over and flatten.

Bigfoot had finished its turn and was heading toward the parked cars. Frank started to run again. He refused to let himself wonder if he could get to Joe in time, just as he ignored the hammering of his heart and the searing pain in his side. The only thing that mattered was putting each leg in front of the other as quickly as possible.

He reached the last of the parked cars as Bigfoot was slowing down, shifting into low gear for its approaching task. Frank started waving his arms over his head, but Bigfoot's driver was staring straight ahead and didn't seem to notice him below.

Frank began to shout, but he knew even as he did that it was useless. All around him, the spectators, sensing that something unusual was going on, were on their feet, yelling. How could one voice possibly be heard over such a racket?

Bigfoot was less than twenty feet away when Frank jumped on the trunk of the first junker to be crushed. He stood there a moment, gasping for breath. The immense ribbed wheels continued to roll toward him, and for one awful moment he was afraid that the driver's view of him was blocked by the truck's hood.

Then Bigfoot stopped, almost on top of him. High above, a helmeted head poked out the side window and a voice shouted, "Are you nuts? Get out of the way. You're blowing my act!"

Frank still didn't have enough breath to shout back. He shook his head, then looked behind him. A dozen Skulls, Fat Dave among them, were going from one junk sedan to another, rapping on the trunk lids. Frank closed his eyes for a moment. What would he do if his hunch about Joe's whereabouts was wrong?

Suddenly there was a gasp from the audience. Frank opened his eyes. Two Skulls with pry bars were forcing open the trunk of a light blue sedan. The lid flew upward, and the audience gasped again, even louder.

A dazed-looking Joe staggered out of the trunk and stood up. Then he turned back to lift Jessica's limp body from the tiny enclosure. Two paramedics came running, stretcher in hand, and took her from him.

Frank glanced upward. Bigfoot's driver was staring at the drama taking place in front of him. He looked ready to faint at the realization of what had almost happened.

Frank walked quickly to Joe's side and put his arm around his brother's shoulders. "I'm glad to see you," he said. "How are you?"

"Glad to see *you*," Joe replied in a shaky voice. "I was starting to wonder if I ever would again!" He glanced around at Bigfoot and shuddered.

Tucker approached the Hardys and listened.

"Do you know who put you and Jessica in there?" Frank asked urgently.

Joe shook his head, then winced. "Ouch," he said, touching a spot just above his ear. "Nope. I never saw him," he continued. "He hit me from behind. But I can make a pretty good guess."

"I have an idea, too," Frank said. "I wonder if it's the same as yours."

"Listen, we've got to go ahead with the final parade," Grant interrupted. "The TV people insist. But afterward, I want this business settled. The thing is, the money isn't mine. I had to borrow it from some guys who have their own ways of collecting."

"We get the picture," Frank said. "We'll do our best."

"Great rescue!" Grant exclaimed. "Just fantastic, and we've got every bit of it on tape."

"Terrific," Joe said sarcastically. "I'd love to view it sometime."

"No problem," the promoter said, and ran off.

Twenty minutes later, as the audience was leaving the arena, Frank, Joe, and all the members of the company gathered backstage in the work area. At each of the exits stood a line of watchful Flying Skulls. Everyone except the Skulls seemed to be talking at once.

Grant Tucker stepped forward, held up his hands, and shouted, "Hey, pipe down!"

Silence fell.

"Okay, thanks," he continued. "You all know about the run of accidents we've been having. And most of you saw what happened tonight, or what almost happened. What you don't know is that somebody has extorted a lot of money from me by threatening to cause even worse accidents."

Ignoring the murmurs among his listeners, Grant said, "Frank and Joe Hardy are detectives. I asked them to join the company to help me catch the extortionist. The best thing I can do now is shut up and let them get on with it."

Frank scanned the faces of the company as they turned to look at him and Joe. Some were interested, even excited. Others seemed to want to get the night over with. One face wore an expression of arrogant confidence, but Frank thought he saw doubt beginning to seep in at the edges.

"One problem we had from the beginning," Frank said, "was figuring out what this case was really about. The extortion, sure, but what else? The accidents? The problems with a certain motorcycle club?"

He paused long enough for some of the Flying Skulls to finish guffawing.

"Or was it all connected? Was somebody in the show working with the Skulls to cause the accidents?" Frank continued.

"Now hold on," said Fat Dave. "I didn't—"

Joe held up his hand. "We had to check out the

144

possibility," he said. "And it didn't help that Jessica had some kind of connection with your bunch. We still don't know what it was."

"She kept coming around, telling us how we had to work with Grant instead of against him," the gang leader replied. "And we couldn't just tell her to get lost. Mike Derey, her father, was one of the founders of the West Coast branch of the Skulls. That carries a lot of weight with us. So we agreed and offered to help keep the crowds under control tonight."

"That's one mystery cleared up," Joe said. "Now we know that was her on the back of your motorcycle the other day, and that the silver helmet we saw at the headquarters was hers. Let's take care of another mystery while we're at it. Keith, what is that Flying Skull tattoo doing on your arm?"

The bikers turned to stare at Keith, who reached up and rubbed the spot where the tattoo was. "Er," he said, "when I was a kid, back in Texas, I used to ride with the Skulls now and then. I wanted to join, but they never let me. Later I moved from bikes to hot rods, but I couldn't remove the tattoo."

Frank nodded. "I thought it must be something like that." Turning to the others, he said, "One thing we noticed right away was that most of the accidents were happening to Bruce and Keith, who were constantly picking fights with each other in public. It looked as though each of them was trying to sabotage the other. And that turned out to be the truth, more or less."

Bruce and Keith both stared at the ground, not meeting the eyes of any of their fellow performers.

"But," Joe said, "a couple of the accidents seemed different. For one thing, they were a lot more dangerous than a loose gearshift knob or a flat tire. Bruce, did either you or Keith put oil on Jessica's jumping ramp the other day?"

"Of course not," Bruce replied.

"But you did know about it," Frank stated. "We saw you wipe it up afterward."

Bruce gave him an angry stare. "Jessica asked me to. She was afraid Morgan would notice it and write something that would damage the show."

"How about the front wheel that came off?" Frank continued.

Bruce reddened and looked away. "Well . . . that's a stunt I worked up a couple of years ago for the pilot of a TV show. It's very tricky, and dangerous, too, but I've practiced it a lot."

"And that runaway four-by-four this afternoon?" Frank pressed. "Was that you?"

"We wouldn't do a thing like that," Bruce insisted. "I told you, I was in my dressing room. I don't care how many guys in black Keith says he saw near Walt's four-by."

"I never said it was you," Keith said loudly, "but I *did* see somebody in black."

"I believe you," Joe said. "Because I saw him myself later, in the parking lot. That was right after he hit Frank over the head. And tonight I caught a glimpse of him, just before he knocked me out and stuffed me into the trunk of that junker."

"*And* made off with the money," Grant added. "Then he's the guy we're after. But who is he?"

Frank took a chance. "It's as clear as black and white," he said. "The guy we're looking for is somebody who was willing to wreck this show, right when it was about to make a breakthrough. Why? Because he hated the thought that other people were going to hit the big time and he wasn't."

Grant shook his head. "I don't get it," he said. "Anything good that happens to our show helps all of us."

"Maybe," Joe said, "but it doesn't help everybody equally. The performers tonight can now say that they've been on coast-to-coast TV. But what about the people who weren't out there? What can they brag about?"

"They can brag about being part of the greatest hot rod, motorcycle, and four-by-four show in the world," Grant said.

Frank nodded. "Sure, but what if you think you should be a star of the show and you're not? You might manage to work up a lot of resentment. You might decide to go after what you think you're owed, no matter what you have to do to get it."

"That's nonsense," said Grant. "Anybody who's got what it takes can be a star in this show. He doesn't have to set up accidents or write extortion notes to do it."

"And if he doesn't have what it takes?" asked Joe quietly. "Or if he used to have it but doesn't anymore?"

Frank let his gaze travel to the face of their number-one suspect. He was pale now, and along the top edge of his forehead, tiny drops of sweat glistened under the bright lights.

"We knew some other things about the extortionist," Frank said. "The extortion note he sent Grant was the work of somebody who could do precise, delicate work. And the way the accidents were set up showed that he could go wherever he liked around the arena without being noticed and that he had a lot of technical knowledge about hot rods. It started to look as if we were after somebody on the crew."

"Now wait a minute," Keith objected. "You were just telling us that this guy thinks he should be a star, and now you're saying he's on the crew. That doesn't jibe. Crew members don't become stars."

That drew some good-natured hoots from members of the crew. When they died down, Frank said, "Maybe not, but what if somebody *was* a star before he became a member of the crew?"

An uneasy silence fell over the huge room.

Frank watched as first one person, then another, and finally everyone turned to look at Matt, who glanced rapidly from side to side.

"Why are you all looking at me?" he said, fiddling with the zipper of his white coverall. "I didn't do anything."

"What are you wearing under your coverall?" Joe demanded. "No, don't bother answering. I know. Black jeans and a black T-shirt."

Matt started to zip the coverall up to his neck. Then he realized what he was doing. "So what?" he said. "Lots of people wear black. Bruce, for instance."

"That reminds me," Frank said. "Bruce, this afternoon, right after the incident with the four-by-four, you saw Matt come out of the toolroom with a timing light in his hand. You said you thought it looked like a pistol. Can you think why?"

Bruce frowned. "No," he said. "No special reason. Just that it was black, and shaped sort of like a pistol, and— Hey, wait. Now I remember. It didn't have the wires coming out of the handle."

"And a timing light has to have those wires to work," Joe stated.

"Why, sure it does," Bruce said. "You need them to hook it up to the ignition system."

"And Matt would know that, wouldn't he?" Frank said. "He wouldn't go to the toolroom for a timing light and not get the wires that go with it—not unless he was in such a hurry that he didn't notice."

"Not unless he had just rushed in and pulled his white coveralls on over his black jeans and shirt," Joe specified.

Matt folded his arms across his chest and said, "You guys don't have a thing on me."

Frank looked down at Matt's feet and said, "Would you mind showing us what's in that toolbox?"

Matt staggered as if he had just been slugged. "Tools, that's all," he gasped. "My own personal tools."

"Open the box," Grant growled. "If Frank and Joe are wrong about you, I guarantee they'll make a public apology. But if they're right . . ."

Matt looked around hastily, as if thinking of making a break for it. Then his shoulders slumped. Bending down, he unlocked the toolbox and raised the lid.

Somebody in the room whistled loudly. The box was filled to the brim with money.

"Everybody, back off!" Grant shouted. "We're not giving out free samples!"

Minutes later, Frank and Joe were sitting with Grant in his office, the money sitting between them on the floor. "You're taking a big risk, letting Matt go like that," Joe said.

"I don't think so," the promoter replied. "He knows if he shows up at the D.A.'s office tomorrow morning, I'll help pay for his lawyer. He's still one of the company, after all. And if he doesn't show, he knows I'll chase him from here to Saskatchewan, and so will the Skulls. What would you do?"

"Good point," Frank said.

"I've got to admit I'm still confused, though," Grant said. "Which accidents were part of Keith and Bruce's act, and which ones did Matt cause?"

"Keith put an extra quart of oil in Bruce's tank Thursday. That's why the engine started smoking," Joe replied. "But Matt admitted pouring the oil on Jessica's jumping ramp and causing Keith's dragster to catch fire. And of course he's the one who aimed the 4x4 at us—the one that had no driver. He claims now that he warned Jessica about the ramp and that he knew Keith's fireproof coveralls would protect him. But I've got the feeling he didn't really care if somebody got hurt. He certainly didn't care about the lump he put on Frank's head, or the danger he put Jessica and I in today when he locked us in that trunk."

Grant sighed. "One more thing. Who's the one who called and left the message that Keith was stranded on the highway?"

"Fat Dave admitted to setting that up himself," Frank replied. "He wanted to send you a message, but he didn't care who actually showed up to get it. Joe and I were the lucky ones."

The telephone interrupted him. Grant picked

it up and talked softly for several minutes, then hung up. "That was the hospital," he reported.

"Jessica?" Joe asked.

"She's okay," the promoter said. "I just spoke to her. She says the doctor thinks she'll be fine in a few days."

"That's a big relief," Joe said. "I still don't understand what she was doing in the garage tonight. Could she have been working with Matt?"

Grant shook his head. "Not on your life! She says she overheard Matt when he called to tell me where to bring the money, and she decided to investigate on her own. She figured she'd take the money and give it back to me so that Matt wouldn't carry out his plan. She thought she could talk Matt out of it, the way she talked Fat Dave out of hassling us."

"She was taking a terrible risk," Frank said. "It almost cost Jessica her life."

"She takes terrible risks all the time," Grant replied. "That's part of her job."

"Taking risks, sure," Joe said. "But not trying to stop crime. That's *our* job."

Grant smiled. "And you're both stars at it, too," he said. "By the way, how would you like some free passes to the show?"

As Frank and Joe were getting into the van to drive home, they suddenly heard a thunderous roar.

"Now what!" Joe exclaimed.

Two long lines of motorcycles came sweeping around the corner of the Bayport Arena. Twenty or thirty of them roared past and came to a halt a little ahead of the van. The rest formed up in back.

One big bike left the pack and pulled up next to the van. Fat Dave grinned at Joe and Frank. "We just want to make sure you boys get home safely," he said. "You never know what you might run into, this late at night."

Frank looked over at Joe and rolled his eyes. "Just wait till we try to explain this to Dad," he said.

"Yeah," Joe replied. "What will the neighbors think?"

THE HARDY BOYS® SERIES By Franklin W. Dixon